THE CONCRETE BOOT

Ossie Jenkins went into the River Thames with his feet cemented into a concrete block.

'Spider' Scott could be the next candidate on Rex Riesen's list for this treatment. He already has a police record and fails in his efforts to go straight as he runs a travel agency in London.

Matters get more complicated . . . a traitor, a snatch job at London Airport, and Spider becomes close to Reisen's attractive secretary, Penny.

THE CONCRETE BOOT

Kenneth Royce

First published 1971
by
Hodder & Stoughton Ltd.

This edition 2002 by Chivers Press
published by arrangement with
Ania Corless

ISBN 0 7540 8619 4

British Library Cataloguing in Publication Data available

Printed and bound in Great Britain by
Bookcraft, Midsomer Norton, Somerset

For Stella

I would like to thank those officials at London Airport who gave me every facility and help.

CHAPTER 1

Ossie Jenkins came floating to the swollen surface of the Thames like a bloated crocodile, distended belly uppermost. His sodden grey suit clung like dripping scales. He floated quite serenely with the current, eyes closed, his many problems at last solved. Ossie had been dead for some days at the muddy bottom of the river where he had joined the waving fronds of weed, his feet cemented in a concrete block, his arms reaching helplessly up to the faint light above him. They had not troubled to kill him first. Ossie had died hard.

There were many witnesses as he silently steered himself head first towards Blackfriars Bridge. There were a few gasps and a couple of small screams before the Thames River Police hooked him out, a dripping mass of lifeless putrescence.

I came into it because the police wanted an identification and poor old Ossie had no known relatives – or none that were forthcoming. Ossie had been a 'creeper' like myself and the record showed that we had once done a joint caper that had not turned out too profitable.

The fuzz dug me out of my new offices just off Trafalgar Square. As usual they made a big thing of it; car, uniforms, formal approaches that must have had my staff wondering. Staff? Well, a young manager in his late twenties, a youngster in his late teens, Dolly, a smart mini-skirted luscious that Maggie wanted me to get rid of, and a typist sharing a partitioned office with me behind the shop counter.

In a quick, quiet aside, I fixed it with the sergeant to call me sir as we went past the three counter staff so they would know the boss was returning and had not been nicked. I went out with the fuzz in a well-practised tread and wondered if I would ever be able to drop the prisoner and escort

7

routine. They held the car door open for me and whipped me off to the morgue.

At first I had a job recognizing old Ossie's putty-puffed face. The sight turned me sick but it was him all right. Ossie wouldn't climb another stack, and I briefly wondered if he had finally descended one; I suppose I would land up in the same place. I uttered a short, crude, mental prayer and hoped Ossie was all right wherever he was right now.

'Who did it?' I asked the sergeant.

'Is it Ossie?'

I nodded, waiting for his answer.

'Who do you think did it?' he tried on me.

'Don't be daft,' I said. 'How did he float up?'

'Some bloody fool put too much sand in the foot clamp. When the water got at it the concrete gradually disintegrated and he popped up like a bubble.'

'Bastards.' I had liked Ossie a lot; he had been a real pro of a creeper and a good bloke.

'Yes, but which bastards?' prompted the copper.

'Don't ask me,' I said, heading for the door.

'There's a whisper that the Reisens did it.'

I turned to look at him. 'Then they're getting bloody careless. And whoever mugged up the concrete mixture will be deep-diving himself if they're behind it.'

I made them drive me back because I'm awkward when it comes to coppers.

On the way I noticed the newspaper placards were full of the searing news that Chapman, the Prime Minister's Parliamentary Private Secretary had escaped from Brixton Magistrates Court after having been arrested only a week or so ago. Hell, this was going to cause the biggest political scandal of all time. I asked the fuzz to drop me near St Martin's in the Field, where I bought an *Evening Standard*. From there I walked the short distance to my place.

In the travel agency two plain-clothes men leaned across the counter talking confidentially to the fair-haired manager, Charlie Hewitt. I came up nice and quiet and said, 'Can I help you?'

The two coppers looked up, and Charlie, who had seen me approach, gave a sickly grin and a sort of introduction, 'This is Mr Scott, the proprietor,' he explained to the coppers. 'These gentlemen are from Scotland Yard, sir. They want to know if this man has travelled through us, and if so to where. I think I recall the face.' Charlie was loving it.

I gazed down at a good photograph of 'Dude' Somers and said, 'He's never travelled through us and if he had I wouldn't tell you.'

Charlie went white and the coppers became interested in me.

'It's not Mr *Spider* Scott by any chance, is it?' As if he didn't know.

'It is,' I said. 'And don't ask *my* staff the movements of *my* clients again. Good day.' I held the door open for them. 'Dude' Somers was one of the Reisens' boys and I was not becoming involved with them.

'You wouldn't want to obstruct the police in their inquiries, would you?' asked the taller one, a sergeant by the look of him.

'Don't give me that. Hop it – gentlemen. Give the Commissioner my regards.'

That threw them a bit. They couldn't be certain that I was joking after the Chinese Legation affair; if they knew of me then they would know about that. They left uncertainly if not a little in awe.

The three counter staff were staring when I turned round. They had seen a side of me which shook them; it was clear I was familiar with the police but I didn't want them to know in what capacity. I headed for the office behind the counter and beckoned Charlie to follow. Lulu was there thumping out on the old typewriter. Sitting down at my desk, I pointed an accusing finger at Charlie.

'Like doctors and solicitors and priests we do *not* divulge the movements or affairs of our clients. Understand?'

He nodded, was about to explain but I stopped him. 'Make sure the rest of the staff know and don't ever do it again, Charlie.'

Seeing my expression he gave up all thought of argument and returned to the counter. In the corner Lulu was still adding her bit for the Noise Abatement Society, so I hid behind the cover of clatter and sat back to think. I'd been a little unfair with Charlie but there was good reason and I couldn't risk it happening again.

I stared round me, at the plumping Lulu with her not quite-matching hairpiece reaching her back, at my own shabby desk, the second-hand map of the world hanging on one wall, at the shadowy forms of the counter staff beyond the frosted glass, and I worked it out.

Fairfax, better known to the public as Sir Stuart Halliman and head of DI5, had virtually offered to fix me a job in DI6 after the Chinese affair. It meant a lot of travelling, immediately, in fact, to Japan. I'd carefully considered it. The pay wasn't enormous but the perks on expenses were good. The job was a doddle for a loner which I was and there seemed to be some excitement attached to it. Yet I had turned it down for a variety of reasons.

I prefer to do my travelling in my own time and to enjoy it. But mainly I turned it down because I did not see myself as a spy. Working alone was one thing; enduring utter loneliness was quite another. They would use me largely for the dirty breaking-and-entering jobs around the globe and I couldn't see myself winning them all and didn't fancy spending years in a foreign nick. I'm a Londoner; if I returned to nick in England I'd at least know a few of the boys. I suppose I'm a sentimentalist.

I don't think Fairfax was all that surprised but then it took a lot to shake him. I smiled a little as I recalled the soldierly figure.

So I went into the travel business. From the seventeen and a half thousand pounds I'd made out of Fairfax and the Chinese I invested fifteen thousand in this small agency near Trafalgar Square and called it XYY TRAVEL. You can't get much in the way of a travel business for that sort of money. I'd met an accountant in Dartmoor and got him to look at the balance sheets; you can guess he's the sort to know what to look for. He wasn't all that keen on my buying but I reckoned I could build it up. The important thing was that it had all the air and shipping licences. It still possessed one or two decent-sized commercial accounts, business-house travel, and there were enough offices and shops around for us to flog a good number of the big tourist boys' package tours. We just about managed and Moggy Morgan the accountant came in twice a week to do the books. Maybe I was asking for it but I trusted him, though I can't say I'd recommend him to anyone else.

I let young Charlie Hewitt have his head in running it – with what I knew I had no option – but I got him to teach me the rudiments. Charlie's one of those youngsters who thinks he is always right, and the trouble is that he is. As it was my own business I set about learning fast but discovered that it was full of pitfalls and I had a hell of a long way to go. I stuck with it.

For some weeks we ticked over, even broke a little the right side but as winter came on the holiday business fell flat and we had to survive on the business-house accounts. It was not enough and the summer profits began to dwindle. By spring we were low on cash.

The take-over price had included four thousand accumulated profits which would hold us for a bit, but I began to wonder if Moggy wasn't right; he began to give me knowing looks from those sunken eyes in his troglodyte's pale, seamed face. The bloody pessimist looked as if he was enjoying it. It was clear, though, that I would have to drum up more business. All my efforts at honest work seemed to revert to salesmanship of one kind or another, but now I was flogging the abstract – there was no commodity to sell, only service, and I'm not exactly the city type.

I found myself doing rather better with the secretaries than the bosses. This was useful if long-term although there were side benefits.

Then business started to increase for quite a different reason; this was good yet dangerous. The word had got round nearby Soho and the 'boys' started drifting in from

London's underworld. 'Spider's in the travel business!' It filtered into all corners; restaurants, shady bars, doss houses and plush hotels. After the last caper a sort of legend had sprung up around me; it was well known I wasn't a grasser, I'd never squealed on anyone. But now they imagined I had pull in high places. Incredible stories floated around and I was viewed with awe by the seamier villains and with respect by the top boys. It was worship I could do without.

So the 'boys' started calling. Their appearance must have frightened Dolly, our touch of brunette glamour, to death when they claimed my friendship and instant service.

Our clientele suddenly became as cosmopolitan as you can get. They made some good bookings, particularly when the heat was on and they had to scarper quick. There was another advantage; most of them hadn't joined the tax club so they paid in cash. It was good business but didn't improve our image. I had a job stopping some of them talking about the old days behind bars in front of the staff, who must have wondered about me, but I looked after them as best I could and they remained loyal. Anyway, there was nothing I could do about the situation. I couldn't refuse the business on economic grounds and some of the 'boys' could be touchy; I didn't want to finish up floating down the Thames like Ossie Jenkins. And it could happen.

So business had picked up but I had problems. Big problems. My agency must have been unique, with the biggest clientele of villains in the business. It was like riding a bomb with a faulty fuse. I didn't feel suicidal enough to turn their business away yet I was becoming involved with people I had tried to break away from. So I lived from day to day and enjoyed the increased profits without losing too much sleep, and jacked up the staff's salaries to keep them on my side. I figured that with four full-time and one part-time on my payroll I had four and a half alibis if ever I needed them.

Dolly brought the afternoon tea and I took a quick look at the midday edition of the *Standard*.

The Chapman case had been a sensation for days but never as sensational as now. Alan Bruce Chapman had been the Prime Minister's Parliamentary Private Secretary until his arrest under the Official Secrets Act. To the justifiable annoyance of the Jewish community Chapman had been nicknamed by the press as Abbie Cee in view of his initials.

The *Standard* looked as though it had been completely taken over by the story. Sixty-point headlines and most of the front page, the leader, an article on prison security, a statement from the Home Office, and a piece underneath a photograph of Chapman's home with the usual 'but he was such a nice man' quotes from the neighbours.

There had been a big security clamp-down on any detail but news of the arrest burst on the nation like a bomb. Chapman had been accused of treason and would know as much as the Prime Minister himself. God help us! The public storm seemed to be gathering while the Government issued the usual idiotic reassurances. The more they played it down the greater the certainty that this case was going to make Burgess, McLean and Philby appear like schoolboys sneaking to teacher by comparison.

Everyone waited. Chapman was remanded in Brixton prison pending further Special Branch inquiries. When he came up to the Magistrates Court for the second remand this very morning he had been sprung. Reading the report now, it was obviously a well-planned, gang job with the clever use of decoys and strong-arm mobsters. Chapman had been whipped away and was still missing. The newspaper was asking if the snatch had been done by a foreign power or by Government sources too embarrassed and afraid to allow the case to reach the open courts? Blimey! The only chance the Government stood of coming out clean was to find Chapman quickly. But Chapman could already be on his way out of the country or pig food.

This was one for Fairfax with DI5, and the Special Branch. I knew the man, respected his ability, so I could feel for him. He was up against it, cagey as he was. I can't stand traitors and I hoped Fairfax and his merry men would win out without seriously believing that they would.

Dolly came in, the hem of her skirt reaching the top of my

desk as if she was standing on it with no legs, collected the cups, looked at the newspaper and said how exciting it all was. I supposed that was one way of looking at it. With the amount of space the story would get in the newspapers and on the radio and television over the next few weeks she would probably be sick and tired of it before too long.

'Oh, and there's a Mr Roberts wants to see you.' As he came through the door I realized with a sinking feeling that it was Knocker Roberts. He had tried to get me to join the Reisens' mob as soon as I had left prison.

'Hello, Knocker,' I said warmly, holding out a big hand. He grinned back, his skin puckering around his left eye where he had received a graft some years earlier. He was dressed flashily with bell bottoms and high-necked coat; his idea of a placid image. Knocker Roberts was as ugly as they come, with thick lips and a mashed face that had once lost out to a mangle. His brown, doglike eyes could evoke tremendous sympathy but in Dartmoor I had seen in them the odd pinprick flashes that denoted the pathological killer. It's something you know and recognize without asking questions. Knocker enjoyed hurting, was always looking for the excuse.

For some reason he liked me and we had been sort of mates on the Moor but I had always known I was treading on eggshells. In spite of his hefty handshake and sincere greeting I was treading them now.

'Sit down, Knocker. Nice to see you. Lulu, can you leave us for a couple of minutes? Old friend,' I explained.

Lulu flounced out, hairpiece flying, and gave Knocker a cutting look which he took good-humouredly. He could be very amusing when he wanted but you were never certain which switch had been turned on that morning. I knew for a certainty Reisen had sent him. One or two of Reisen's boys had been booking these last few days, which made me nervous.

We talked for a bit; the Moor, the quarries, this prison warder and that, coppers. To Knocker all screws and coppers were bastards. He squinted at me through his puckered eye and I could see that he was leading up to why he had

14

called. His coarse, huge hands twisted nervously. Messenger-boy was not Knocker's metier; he was an action man, happier knocking the life out of someone.

'The boss asked if you would like to drop by and see him.'

'Asked?'

Knocker grinned. 'You know Reisen, me old mate. He wants to see you.'

'That's better. Tell him, no. Not interested, whatever it is.'

Knocker had been primed and it struggled out. 'You've got it wrong, whack. It's business. Your kind.'

'And what kind's that?' I'd given up creeping.

'What's the matter with you?' Knocker was getting aggrieved. 'This bloody business here, ain't it? Travel business.'

I sighed with relief. 'Keep your voice down, Knock, the staff will hear you.' Then I saw the trap. 'It would be better if he came here, spoke to Charlie Hewitt. All the reference books are here.'

'You know he won't speak to anyone else. You don't need any bloody books. When he's talked you can hand it over to Charlie what's-his-name then, can't you? Now cut it out, Spider. Stop being awkward or I'll get stroppy.'

It was not so much of an invitation from Reisen as a Royal Command. But he had asked Knocker to set about it nicely. That meant a *friendly* talk otherwise he would have sent a second man and merely issued an instruction.

It was awkward. I wanted no part of Reisen – he was poison. But I didn't want his wrath either. Knocker had been sent because I knew him but also because he was a psychological reminder of violence – intimidation. Knocker might look like an array of baked potatoes with their jackets on, but he was no fool; his animal mind was sharp. He hadn't come to hear a refusal; he'd been told to soft soap but to get me over there.

'About travel, you say.' I played for time.

'Sure. Wants a holiday in winter. Bahamas or somewhere like that.'

15

I'd just about discovered where they were. 'O.K. Where and when.'

Knocker relaxed. Being tactful had been hard on him. 'Off Old Compton Street. The Club. Side door. Six o'clock. OK? See you, whack.'

When Knocker left Lulu returned and eyed me disapprovingly. She had lashes painted round her very attractive blue eyes, spoiling them, but she worked hard. She sat down at the old machine I would soon have to replace and banged out the mail and itineraries.

Maggie had reluctantly gone on a long cruise with her parents. I suppose she owed it to them; anyway they had paid for it, making it almost impossible for her to refuse. After the strain on her over the last business she needed it.

Maggie was the only person in the world I trusted. Because she was from a good family, it always amazed people, and me in particular, that she stayed with me. I had told her often enough that with her looks she could do far better for herself than waste her time on me but she stuck it out whatever I did. I had tried to shock her into breaking with me for her own sake but there were times when I had thanked God she had not.

So I had no evening commitments which I could use as an excuse to ring Reisen and politely call it off. Even if I did he'd nail me some other time.

I was the last to leave, just after half five. It was spring and warm with only light tufts of yellow cloud hanging below a very blue sky. The white cross on the red flag of the Swiss Centre strung out behind the dome of the National Portrait Gallery as if it were fixed to wire. Traffic moved slowly. The placards were still full of Chapman.

Taking my time, I crossed into a crowded Leicester Square, cut across the green and reached Coventry Street, heading towards the bleak shallow canyon of Lisle Street. Past the electrical spare parts shops, into the fringe of new Chinatown and up to and across Shaftesbury Avenue, the theatre district. Then into Soho, spice, spaghetti and strip-club land. One or two of the boys nodded, and I searched for the club. It wasn't difficult to find. Glossies of busty nudes reclined behind glass panels. The strip club belonged to Reisen although it would be a job proving it. The plain door was beside the club at the short end of some green railings.

I rang the bell and a voicebox crackled in my ear. I told him who I was and pushed the door. Inside it was well lit and carpeted and the stairs went straight up so I followed them. On the first landing two of Reisen's thugs stopped me pleasantly and gave me a thorough frisking. When you're a Reisen you never know who your enemies are. I was told to go up the next flight. Three plain white doors faced me on the second landing; before I could move one opened and Knocker Roberts stepped out.

'Bang on time, whack. He'll like that. Come in, mate.'

It was a plush waiting-room; light leather armchairs, a couple of genuine Canterburies with magazines and papers, ashtrays on stands, thick carpeting and some pleasant original oils hanging from the walls. The mixed décor screamed mess and I guessed that it reflected Reisen's own taste. But the chairs were comfortable. Knocker disappeared and I thumbed through *The Times*. *The Times* – who was Reisen kidding!

There are two Reisens. The elder is a cousin and stays largely in the background and is seldom seen, almost a recluse. Yet the word is that it is he who is the really tough egg, makes the real decisions. I don't know; I wouldn't like to gamble on it. The younger, Rex Reisen, was more than tough enough for me and most of the rumours of killings centred around him.

I was just getting interested in the share prices and the market index when a very striking bird came in. Her neat tailored suit was beige, the skirt not too high above interesting knees, and her long nails on slender soft white fingers had never thumped a keyboard like Lulu's did. Yet she had the air of a superior secretary and I wondered how Reisen had managed to get her on the payroll. Dark hair was swept up from a long slender neck that gave her elegance. She said, 'Mr Scott?' in so polite and charming a fashion that for a moment I forgot where I was. She had nice hazel eyes, a pale skin, lips firm and smiling, nose a little snub. She would not have won a beauty contest but she would have left the other competitors behind in poise and charm. Her gaze as I rose was steady and there was something in it that disturbed me, something I felt I should have recognized. There was no time for more, for she was ushering me into another office.

It was huge. Two or three rooms had been knocked into one. It was the office of a rich man, a man with little taste. The desk was an antique partner's desk, magnificent, completely spoiled by a nightmarish mauve patterned wall-to-wall carpet. Each wall was a different pastel shade; the ceiling had been corniced and two lovely chandeliers hung ludicrously above tubular chrome chairs and modern black swivel armchairs. Modern paintings jibed the crystal droppers. Well, it was Reisen who had to live with it.

Cutting my way through the foliage of the carpet I approached the man in the far distance, who was almost lost behind his desk. My first impression of Reisen as he rose was mediocrity and I quickly discarded it as the most dangerous thought of the day. Medium height in a well-cut light grey suit, he approached, hand extended, smiling affably. He was bald on top but his side hair was tinted jet black and he grew his sideburns long and thick to compensate. Brows were dark, the restless brown eyes sunken with deep shadows under them matched by ruts in his very narrow face running down to his chin which suggested privation or strain; it had to be the latter. He eyed me like a benevolent fox.

He shook hands with me as if I was the one person he had wished to meet all his life. He had presence and a little of its evil reached me like a frozen finger on my spine. Reisen was handling something he had handled a hundred times before; it was all under control. He never doubted that whatever he wanted of me I would provide; he was playing rich uncle to his favourite nephew. When he spoke he crushed part of the image but produced part of another, more unsavoury. He should have taken elocution lessons instead of fashioning his accent on the sewers of the world.

'Good of you to come, Spider. Sit down, boy, anywhere you like. Have a cigar.'

I sat near to the desk as I don't like shouting over distances. I shook my head. 'Don't smoke, Mr Reisen.'

'Rex.' He waved his own cigar like a cutlass. 'Rex, boy. We're all in the same game, ain't we? Let's start as we mean to go on. Drink?'

Again I shook my head. It didn't worry him; someone had done his homework for him. 'I heard you didn't smoke and rarely drink. I don't believe in pushing a man.'

Like hell he didn't. He was completely at ease but I wasn't.

'Good move that, starting in the travel business, Spider. Good cover.'

It was a bad start by implication. 'I intend to make it pay,' I said.

'Why, of course, boy. What else? I've been sending some of my boys down to push up your figures.'

'Thanks. I believe you want to go to the Bahamas?'

He pulled on his cigar and thought a bit. 'Yep. That's right. Put a bit of business your way. Then again, you can help on something else.'

Ignoring the second part which had tightened my stomach nerves, I prompted, 'When do you want to go?'

'Time for that,' he said grinning; he had extremely good small white teeth. 'Get one of your boys to send me some leaflets. There's a little job you can do for me. Very simple. You could do it with one arm in a sling.'

'Go on,' I invited, my strength falling from me.

'I want you to break into a house.'

CHAPTER 2

'I've given it up,' I said.

'An empty house,' he added.

'I'm still retired,' I said.

He laughed, using his cigar as a baton. 'In our game, boy, you never retire. Don't start scruples on me, Spider. None of us can afford them. Once you're in, you're in, boy, for all time.'

I tried another tack. 'Why not get one of your own boys to do it if it's so simple?'

'Oh, it's dead simple all right. Not really your class at all. But I don't want my boys to know of this particular jaunt. Also, I'm hoping that you'll become one of my boys but it's mainly because I trust you. There, I've never met you before and yet I trust you. What do you think about that?'

'I think I don't want to go back to nick.'

'Nick? Who mentioned jail? In the first place, it will be the easiest job you'll ever pull, in the second I know you have friends in high places.' He smiled and winked knowingly. 'I like your style, Spider, boy. You don't think we believed that crap the newspapers put out, do you? You've got pull, boy, the McCoy. I've talked to Balls Up and Bluie Palmer. They're loyal to you, I give them that, but I'm not stupid. You had the twist on someone, that's a fact, so what's all this about nick?'

Balls Up and Bluie had better be loyal. Fairfax had threatened them with the Official Secrets Act if they uttered a word.

'I'm not doing it,' I said flatly. I didn't feel so brave.

His eyes were still bright, as if suddenly polished. The grin was lopsided and frozen like the cigar halfway to his mouth.

He appeared almost moronic but I knew his little mind was darting all round his narrow cranium and that sort of brain knew where to find the dark holes. While he was figuring it out I tried to look around.

Behind Reisen's desk was a long shelf below the window on which were a group of photographs with a Union Jack on a chrome stand. I had heard about these. They had been taken in the Middle East during the last war and depicted groups of soldiers in shorts and steel helmets, stripped to the waist, legs bare. In one they were grouped round a tank, in another round a field gun and yet another holding rifles. The photos were bad, shadow falling over faces almost down to their chins. By implication Reisen was one of the soldiers. In the very centre, encased in a velvet frame, was a military medal complete with ribbon. Again, the implication was that it was Reisen's. I knew better, for I too had done my homework.

Reisen had never seen the Middle East except as a tourist long after the war. He had been called up in 1940 and had somehow worked his ticket into the Catering Corps. And there he had stayed, never leaving the United Kingdom, and starting his first big racket by flogging Army food on the black market.

Yet he was a patriot in a queer way. I heard he was genuinely all for Queen and Country – even if he didn't reckon the law of the land had been made for him – but he had lacked the guts to be the hero he always dreamed himself to be. So he created impressions like the photos and the medal and references to the war days. To support this fearless image of himself he climbed up the back passage of life to notoriety as a substitute for heroism. If he killed a man then it was from behind his back; or his money bought someone else to do the dirty work.

Reality overlapped wishful thinking. He no longer knew the truth himself. An unstable man. Like an old .38 with the barrel worn, the ratchet on the cylinder gone and the trigger pressure far too light, he was both highly unpredictable and deadly. He could go off at any moment, which is often the case with men who daily have to assert themselves with a mixture of self-hypnosis, lies and aggression. A wrong word could ignite him; these days he had learned to use the slow fuse, which only made the result more certain. He used it now. Slowly he released himself from frigidity; the smile continued, the arms functioned. He tapped off his ash so he didn't have to eye me immediately. Then he leaned back expansively; Uncle Rex was about to pronounce.

'Look, boy, I'm doing you a favour. I've been trying to help you all along. Look at the business I'm sending down. And that's not all, Spider. I have large legit businesses, big stuff. One word from me and they book their travel through you, boy, just like that.'

I knew it to be true. I hesitated. 'What's with this empty house?' I asked, mainly to placate him.

He grinned, thinking he had victory. 'Well, there's nothing to it. Look, I merely want to use it for transit for a short time. There are draught excluders running outside the doorframe so you can't use mica on the lock. I don't want a visible job or we could tear them off. But for that any of my boys could do it. All I want you to do is get in nice and clean and put the front door on the latch. That's all. Nothing to nick, nothing to pinch you for.'

'Except breaking and entering,' I murmured mildly.

'Come off it, boy. *You* with your class. Look, I'll sling in a hundred. How's that? I'm chucking it away.'

He was too. And that worried me more than anything else. A hundred pounds, plus an offer of the travel business from his many interests was far too generous. Reisen would keep his word because he couldn't bear to lose face. In a perverted way his word was his bond; until he decided that your contract was terminated and then he served notice with a bullet in the back of the head or some other more painful way.

I was a nut even to consider it, but Reisen had the crackers nice and firmly round me. He could do the business a power of good. I dreaded to think what he might do to it if I turned him down once again. And the extra Y chromosome in my make-up was working for him instead of me. I should explain that while in prison the medicos discovered that I had an extra Y chromosome which gave me a compulsion towards crime of the non-violent type; it was difficult to beat.

'And it's as easy as you say?'

'You're a suspicious bugger, Spider. But I like that, that's sense. Look, I'll get Knocker to run you down tomorrow, OK? You can see for yourself.'

Before I could reply he had risen and moved over to a modern cabinet, which after a button was pressed, opened out into an enormous drinks cabinet, all coloured glass and harsh lights reflecting everywhere. The chandeliers dimmed in shame.

'How's Maggie?' he threw over his shoulder. 'When's she due back?'

The bastard. It was a threat. Just in case I needed one. But he was all smiles and Spider, Spider, when he insisted that I had one small drink for the road.

On the way back to my place I reflected that if ever it came to the point there would be at least a dozen people who would swear that I had not been there that evening and that Reisen had been elsewhere. Some of those immediately around him were people without form so that their testimony could not be ridiculed in court. I wondered how the girl stood in this. Would she perjure herself for Reisen? I didn't fancy her chances if she didn't.

Knocker turned up at the office at ten thirty next morning. Lulu gave me one of her dirty looks when I went outside with him. I think that at the ripe age of nineteen she was trying to keep a motherly eye on me. Knocker's blood-red DBS V8 was parked on double yellow lines.

It's strange but whenever I'm with Knocker I always manage to get his screwed-up side like a glass eye in crushed foil. I got it now as he climbed behind the wheel. I was beginning to surround myself with the type of villain I had sworn I would avoid. But at the moment it seemed the lesser of two evils; they could do my business a great deal of harm or good as the mood took them. I wouldn't like any of his boys near my ticket stocks.

As Knocker drove nice and steadily through the traffic, giving all the right road signals to avoid the risk of any minor charges, I took a good look at his sideface. He had served in Korea and came out with a good Army record. It wouldn't surprise me if the medal for valour in Reisen's office was Knocker's. It was somehow strange that the underworld included a good many deserters but some heroes too; men who couldn't stand the routine rat race of civilian life, but then found themselves trapped by a bigger rat race of their own creation. Knocker would have turned to crime because it offered more opportunity to hurt people. And to be able to hurt *and* make money from it was his idea of heaven.

He drove us to an area bordering North and South Kensington. It was a quiet residential street of three-storied Edwardian houses with bay fronts and sash windows. He found a parking spot and skilfully slipped the car into it.

'Over there,' he said without moving his head.

I was supposed to understand his direction but it wasn't too difficult. A sign was on the iron railings of the small garden. FOR SALE. APPLY A. NOLE AND COMPANY. ESTATE AGENTS AND SURVEYORS. The easiest way to get in would be to ask to view the house but I could understand Reisen not wanting any of his boys to be seen in so obvious a move. The house was on a corner of an intersection. The windows looked blankly back at us and the paintwork was beginning to peel.

I wondered how long it had been empty. Admittedly the area was dull, verging on dingy but the site looked quite good. I wondered about something else too; if Reisen didn't want his boys in on this particular jaunt why have Knocker bring me here?

I climbed out of the car. 'I'm taking a look,' I said and left Knocker sitting there, eyeing his front like a guardsman. Crossing the road I walked past the house slowly and down the intersection, then came back. It certainly seemed as easy as Reisen had said.

Back at the car we sat there like a couple of cons slipping

words out side-mouthed without actually looking at each other.

'With the sort of organization Reisen's got, why me?' I asked reasonably.

'Reisen doesn't carry creepers, you know that, whack. We're on the gang jobs not these solitary larks.'

'You don't need a creeper to break in there, Knock. A kid could do it with a nail file.'

'Yeah, well look, I put a word in for you, Spider. You were good to me in nick. We were good mates, weren't we?'

He turned his head aggressively as if afraid I would say no. I nodded slowly. 'Yes we were.' It was true but the sort of word he had put in I could do without. The fact was that Knocker was genuinely fond of me. I had attempted to straighten him out in nick until I had seen those odd flashes that told me he could not be straightened. You don't desert a man for·that. But we weren't in stir now. Knocker had returned to old habits and I was trying to throw them.

I weighed the pros and cons, then took an oblique look at the house.

'When does he want me to do it?'

'Tonight, mate. Sooner the better.'

'Tell him it's OK.'

Knocker grinned and it was a pity, for his coarse ugliness was less noticeable in repose.

'That's more like it,' he breathed. 'I was getting worried about you. That's my Spider.'

We took off back to the office where the staff must have noticed that I wasn't my usual self for the rest of the day. I could hear them discussing the Chapman case and this added to my irritability.

It was impossible to escape his name. Every newspaper carried banners on him; every time television was switched on his mug shot would come bouncing out of the screen, and he had been reported having been seen up and down the country. The police had already investigated well over a thousand sightings but hadn't produced him yet. On the streets, on tubes and buses, his name thumped out at you, verbally or in print. Right now it was all anyone talked about.

I was still living in the room near Notting Hill which I'd had since I came out although I was half-heartedly searching around for something better. That evening while I relaxed in my favourite chair, the only one worth sitting on, I considered Reisen's offer ridiculously high and it made me very queasy. Reisen paid very fair rates but was not known for giving it away. Another aspect worried me. I was looking forward to it; I shouldn't have been. Buying the agency and then trying to improve it had taken up time and energy and I had not missed the old life. Now, as I prepared my gear I realized that there would always be part of me that wanted it. Anyway, I needed the exercise; I was putting on too much weight.

I caught a bus to a point near the empty house then walked the rest of the way. In the old days I would have nicked a car but I was keen on keeping my crime figures down. It was well before midnight and there was still plenty of movement. I walked down the long road of Edwardian houses and smelled the faint air of mordant decay. The district was shabbier at night, chewed up and ultimately due for the chop. There were fewer people down here and the old tingle in my veins came creeping back.

I found myself a nice deep doorway in the intersection and stood in it for perhaps half an hour with an eye on the house. During that time one or two people passed; they didn't see me. I then crossed the main road and stood in another doorway so that I could watch the front of the house for the same length of time. The ultra caution was due to the absurdity of the whole thing. The only reason I was doing it at all was to keep Reisen off my back.

By now it was after midnight and the street was empty for several minutes at a time. I did not expect trouble; there was the sort of run-down respectability here that would keep the fuzz away. And yet something was holding me back. All the warning signals were flashing in my head, yet I could not believe that Reisen had set me up; he had no reason to.

26

Crossing the road, I opened the iron gate with my lacquered fingertips and let myself into the box of a garden. It was musty and overgrown and hadn't been tended for months. The smell of rotting vegetation reached me. From habit I gently pushed at the front door but it was locked all right. If it hadn't been I would have scarpered.

There was a cracked concrete path round the side of the house, bordered by an unkempt privet hedge that was trying to brush me back against the side of the house. It was narrow but secluded and I trod carefully to avoid the loose chippings, catching myself wondering why I was taking so much precaution when there was no one inside.

I left the back door alone for they are usually bolted from the inside. A quick flash of the torch through the kitchen window revealed a rotting wooden draining-board and an old chipped sink directly beneath the sill. I didn't fancy either would take my fourteen and a half stone so I studied a brick lean-to under a bathroom window. It was no problem getting on to the low corrugated roof and even less trouble slipping the window catch with a clasp knife. Even then I had taken the precaution of checking for alarms, which was a bit of a laugh in a district like this. Lifting the sash window I eased my tall frame through, panting a little, showing how out of training I was; breathing carries a long way. I closed the window behind me and used my torch discreetly.

The bathroom was shabby, paper stripping from the walls and the enamel on the bath chipped. On a ledge above a cracked washbasin was a worn-down shaving brush like an old Army issue, an almost used tube of toothpaste with a worn bristle brush. A safety razor in a discoloured plastic box was set apart with a stub of shaving soap. From habit I felt the ends of the brushes and they were quite dry. From the state of the toiletry I was not surprised that the owner hadn't taken them with him when he moved. The sink basin had globules of water in it but as the tap was still dripping I was not surprised.

I stood on the bare boards of the landing in total darkness

for a few moments listening to the groaning woodwork and throwing a careful ear for any sound beyond it. The house felt empty all right but the strange thing about emptiness, particularly in the dark, is its menace, the threat of unpleasant surprise. Personally I prefer a house that's lived in, then I know my enemy.

I went down the stairs at the side. Woodwork in so old a house invariably creaks where nails have worked loose over the years. In the empty hall on the ground floor suffused light filtered in from the square of thick glass set in the door. It threw a faint patch on the floorboards. A door led off either side of the hall.

At the front door I turned the knob of the Yale lock and slipped up the catch. Gently pulling at the door, I tested it. It didn't budge. The weather was too dry for the wood to be swollen so I had to resort to my carefully shielded torch. There was a bolt top and bottom. I eased them back making no noise. Now that was interesting and very, very disturbing. There was only one way to check out.

From the hall I went down a short passage by the side of the stairs to the kitchen door. I went in, examined it briefly, then studied the back door. There was a key in the lock and a small brass bolt applied low down. I tried the key; it was locked.

Standing with my back to the kitchen door I tried to sort it out. I've run into too many crises in houses to panic but even so I had to quell an urge to run. Both outside doors bolted from the inside could only mean that there was someone in the house.

Should I leave it like this? If I did when I reported back to Reisen he would want to know why I hadn't investigated on the spot. It could be a tramp or a couple of lovers tucked away on the upper floor. He would want to know. And I wanted to know for a different reason.

I crept back up the stairs and opened the bathroom window, leaving the door open so that with the front door on the catch I now had two escape hatches.

When operating silently in existing silence you add something to it like an elecric charge so that it can reach a point when you think the silence will explode as tension increases. I wanted to get out quickly but was too well-trained to make a shabby search.

There was nothing downstairs so I tried the first floor. The rooms had been stripped bare, the floorboards scrubbed. Apart from a general dowdiness the place was very clean. I went up the last flight with a sense of resignation yet no less alert.

I opened the first door on the landing and my hackles rose. In this room there was a camp bed neatly made up with sheets and blankets. The room was otherwise empty. Quickly I spun round to face the other two small rooms on this floor. They were empty. My pulse rate had risen and the alarms were clanging in my head.

Puzzled, I went back to examine the camp bed. The sheets were very slightly crumpled as if they had been used but there was no indentation in the pillows; nobody had jumped out of bed and hidden at my approach, for the bed could never have been made so tidy in the time. Across the room, I found a built-in wardrobe too shallow to hide anyone; it was barely a long cupboard. One door was ajar and I slowly pulled it open. There were hooks at the back on a few of which were wire hangers of the type you get from dry cleaners. On one hanger was a jacket.

I took it down and examined it. It was a well-cut but fairly old grey striped city jacket. The pockets were completely empty, the linings of them more grey than white. I turned down the edge of the inside breast pocket. There was the tailor's label and the date the suit had been made; it was six years old. There was something else in the label; the type had faded but nevertheless I could see it; the owner's name, Alan Bruce Chapman.

Christ! I turned with my back to the wall as if expecting an attack from all sides. Again I looked at the label but there was no miraculous change of name. The Prime Minister's Parliamentary Private Secretary, currently the hottest name in the country.

The most terrifying thought was that Chapman, if he was here at all, was somewhere in the house. He had to be, with both outside doors bolted from inside and all windows locked except the one I had forced. He had to be here.

There was only one place left to look. I stepped out on to the landing and slowly raised my torch. To the left of the attic hatch was one of those retractable ladders which lower when a cord is pulled. He had to be up there waiting, listening, wondering and in fear. That fear had probably armed him with a blunt instrument to stove my skull in if I was stupid enough to push my head into the attic.

I may detest traitors but I've a great regard for my own skin. With the sort of sentence he was likely to get if caught, murder would not increase the years. Chapman had nothing to lose and even if he hadn't played cricket for the old school he couldn't have missed me as my head popped up. So I silently called him all the bastards on the face of the earth and crept down to the first landing.

No trap. No one in sight. Bathroom door still open, window raised. All too good to be true. I didn't trust it. Stepping through the window and on to the low roof raised my spirits and by the time I reached ground level I felt a lot better.

I crept round the side of the house as if I was on a demonstration course; movement and breathing exactly right and eyes revolving all round my head. Still nothing. I peered over the gate to find the street empty, so empty that it was easy to believe there was a copper hiding in every recessed doorway. I walked smartly out of the gate.

There's a time for running and this wasn't one of them but the urge was strong because it was all so odd.

I looked back. The house was still dark; no little gnomes suddenly appeared by candlelight. Yet *someone* was there; the damned house couldn't lock itself.

That night I walked a good distance. I couldn't tie in Reisen with what had happened because I couldn't see any possible point. If he knew Chapman was there he would hardly send me. Just the same, as late as it was, Reisen was going to know, whatever his wrath.

It was now one forty-five – early for Reisen, who would be at one of his casinos. I searched for the nearest phone booth, angry at this stage and more than a little alarmed.

Reisen saw me in the office where I had first met him. He had a tumbler half full of Scotch in one hand and a baton of a cigar in the other. The red tie on the pale lemon shirt looked hideous. I wondered what effect he had on his custo- mers in the gaming rooms. His doglike eyes were warm and friendly and he seemed in a good mood.

'I'm sorry to rake you out,' I said. 'I thought it important enough, that's all!'

'Don't worry about it, boy. Sit down.'

But I had edged beyond his desk to peer at the photographs. 'Which one is you?' It was a dangerous question but I wanted to see how he reacted. I was disappointed.

He grinned as if he'd been through it all a hundred times. 'Can't you see?' he countered.

They were so bad close up that I doubt if anyone could be picked out. He was safe with these. I pointed to one of the shadowed faces. 'This one?'

'You're nearly right,' he said. 'Those were the days. Before your time. Come on, Spider, you didn't come for that.'

Sitting myself in front of him again his face seemed browner than this morning.

'I did what you asked,' I said. 'The front door is on the catch. By the way, I take it you know that someone is living there?'

His gaze sharpened. 'What d'you mean?'

'There's a camp bed set up and a jacket hanging in the wardrobe.'

I was watching him intently and the process of those almost liquid eyes solidifying was unnerving. I had touched a nerve. His eyes were now like pieces of mineral put through a tumbling machine. There was something unsettling in the way he had focused on a spot somewhere between the two of us. He was looking in my direction but his hardened gaze fell short of me as if his sight could only reach so far.

'My information is that the place is stripped bare. What are you trying to give me, Spider?'

'Your information is wrong,' I said. 'Both doors were bolted from the *inside*.'

'Christ!' He was stiff with concentration. Then suddenly his gaze was released from its lock and like a beam swept over and through me. I had the feeling that he was inside my head scrabbling around for the truth. I was learning something about Reisen by the second and liked none of it.

'Christ!' he said again. 'That's bitched it. I can't use it now.' And then, 'Did you see who it was?'

'Whoever it is is in the attic, at least he was while I was there. As I didn't fancy tomato ketchup all over the landing I kept my head where it was. But I know who it is. Alan Bruce Chapman.'

At first the name passed over his head. Then slowly he rose half out of his chair, stooping, glaring at me in a maniacal way that made my sweat glands work. 'What did you say?'

'Alan Bruce Chapman,' I repeated.

'You mean that bastard pimp of a traitor?'

'Unless there's another one.'

'There'll be only one like that on the run. Holed up there?' Reisen sat down again, glaring at me as if I was responsible. 'God help you if you're lying.'

I chilled. I began to be sorry that my attitude with him was casual; but I wasn't one of his men and that's the way I intended it to stay. He would feed on my fear if he saw it. 'If you thought I was a liar you wouldn't have sent me there in the first place.'

His glare didn't diminish and I wondered where the dog-soft brown eyes had gone. The two deep runnels in his face were darkly etched as if his narrow face had sunken farther beneath the high cheek-bones. I was beginning to understand why Reisen stayed on top. 'No,' he murmured quietly. 'You're right.'

Suddenly he swivelled in his chair and pointed vehemently at the little Union Jack on its chrome stand. 'To think that a treacherous bastard like Chapman can disgrace that great flag and all it stands for.'

It was difficult to grasp that this was Britain's top mobster speaking and not someone touting for a by-election. What struck me most was that Reisen meant it; he was incensed. Incredible as it seemed, his allegiance to the flag must have been one of his few sincere pieces of rhetoric. It was all right to beat the system but not to deface the flag. I recalled that this man had sent a team of cleaners down to St Martin's Lane to scrub Nurse Edith Cavell's statue because he reckoned that the council hadn't kept it clean enough. One patriot honouring the memory of another. This fantastic, delicately balanced man was so upset by Chapman's treason that he could hardly speak. The scales of his mind tipped too easily on either side for me to draw comfort from it. Yet the inconsistency of it all worried me. I didn't care for the co-incidence; not with Reisen involved. Wanting to be away, I rose to go.

'Sit down,' he snarled, his eyes reforming under some gigantic thought that began to portray cunning.

He went over to the flag and picked it up. 'A lot of good men have died for this.' For a moment I thought he was going to stand to attention to salute it. But instead he put it down and picked up the framed medal, glowing over it. 'They were tough days, Spider, tough.' He was being less sincere now but not consciously; the rot of self-delusion was rooted too deeply.

Returning to the desk he eyed me intently but a shade more warmly. 'We'll fix him, Spider. People like you and me don't grass, eh? But this is different. This will be like treading on a snake's head and keeping the foot down. You feel the same, eh?'

I did, so I nodded.

'Good,' he said. 'I'll see that the Special Branch get to

know pretty dam' quick.' He grinned like he was watching torture and enjoying it. 'They won't know it came from me. I promise you.'

CHAPTER 3

One thing was certain. As much as I loathed people like Chapman I couldn't ring the police myself or Reisen would suspect me if they raided. Let him do it in his roundabout way.

He did. And he rang me at the office next morning to tell me that the fuzz were going to raid the house at eleven o'clock. I didn't ask him how he knew the timing.

I took a cab to the Kensington area then walked the last few hundred yards. It was as well that the office ran without me.

Knocker's red DBS V8 stood out like a blood clot among the shabby line of cars. I climbed in beside him.

'It's a bit conspicuous, isn't it, if Old Bill* is coming?'

'That's right, whack. When I'm using this it means I don't mind being seen, I'm not on a job. Why? Are you nervous?'

Ignoring the taunt I focused on the house. 'Is Reisen down here watching the fun?'

Knocker screwed his face and the foil crinkled again. 'Don't be stupid.'

So Knocker was acting as Reisen's eye; to see if I came or to see the raid?

The police closed in right on time. They did it well. Plain cars and vans; no sirens or flashers, few uniforms. Properly briefed, they took up positions in the two streets around the house and in the small garden. Then a few of them approached the front door. They had no trouble getting in and I wondered if the door was still on the catch.

Knocker lit a cigarette and stared straight ahead. He was

* Police.

34

relaxed and casual; I wondered if beneath it he was as tense as I was. The police were a long time. The cars were dispersed along the street and there was not too much sign of police activity outside the house, but they were there, a hell of a lot of them and there would be some big brass among them.

'I wish I had a bloody bomb, Spider. I'd get shift of that lot.'

I didn't have the same feeling so I sat and waited and hoped that they would soon bring Chapman out. A good half hour later they reappeared on the doorstep. No Chapman. I sat forward. There had to be. Unless Chapman had heard me in the house but my vanity rejected that possibility.

The small group of plain-clothed officers who had searched the house stood huddled on the pavement, talking, looking up at the neighbouring houses, wondering what to do next. The grapevine had worked fast and people were drifting out of houses and leaning out of windows to watch. Police asked some of them questions while others searched the garden.

It was true that I hadn't actually seen Chapman, but the bed had been there so what had happened to that? The fuzz had brought out nothing, not even the jacket I had seen.

'Reisen's not going to like this, matey,' said Knocker regretfully, not looking at me. 'He's very touchy about this.'

'Reisen can get stuffed,' I said, anger mounting. 'Do you think I invented it all?'

Knocker grunted noncommittally. 'It's not what I think that matters, whack, is it?' He switched on the engine. 'I'll put in a word for you.'

'That's big of you. You forget I don't work for Reisen.'

'And you, ole mate, ole mate, forget that you just have.'

His cruel hands took the wheel and he pulled out into the road, his close-cropped hair forming a ridiculously spiked halo as the sun caught and electrified it.

The police were still grouped as we passed them and I could see something of their bitterness. The only answer was that Chapman must have seen me and pulled up anchor.

In spite of my offhandedness with Knocker, I was worried. Reisen wouldn't find it funny. One thing no one could do to Reisen was to make a monkey out of him and get away with it. I could be straight with Knocker because I knew him but it could literally be fatal to forget that he was one of Reisen's men. I'm big enough and not underpowered for my size but I wouldn't fancy my chances with Knocker. I hated violence and he thrived on it; he was tough, solid, and dirty.

The next two days nothing happened at all, which made things much worse for my jangled nerves. Wherever I went I kept sharp eyes about me, using every trick I knew. I wasn't followed. It was within Reisen's character to keep me dangling like this until I became a nervous wreck or simply got careless.

Four days later Knocker called in, gave Lulu a lecherous grin which he knew would scare her and told me to drop in on Reisen that night. As he didn't linger for a chat I thought that this was it. I didn't have to go, of course. But I would be fetched and that might be painful. All in all, it would be easier to go.

When I reached Reisen's place that evening I was put through the same procedure as before. I bore with it and went into the waiting-room. When I was finally shown in it was by a man and I was briefly disappointed not to have seen the girl who had appeared before.

Reisen was in the distance down by the window. I must admit I felt nervous about the sort of greeting I would get, nor was I fooled by the fact that we were alone together in the room.

He walked towards the desk, narrowing the distance between us, opened a drawer without looking up, took something from it as I got ready to move, then tossed a packet on the desk.

'You forgot to collect your hundred for the job, Spider. All used notes ready to spend.' Reisen was smiling, knowing he had me going, the crevices down his face deepening to hatchet marks. I began to relax cautiously.

36

'Come and sit down,' he called. 'Pity about that bastard Chapman. I'd like to have put the fix on him. Must've seen you.'

Well, well. I went and sat and picked up my money, reckoning that at this stage I'd earned it. I tried a different chair but there was no real comfort in them and Reisen looked the same evil little bugger from any angle. As a matter of principle and to show him that I'd recovered my nerve I counted the notes carefully and stuck them away.

'Don't you trust me?' He hadn't liked what I'd done.

'It's your accountant I'm checking on. If it hadn't been right then he'd have been diddling us both.'

'Smart,' he conceded, not really convinced. 'Has business been coming down to you from some of my interests?'

He knew the answer fine but I let him hear it from me.

'It's beginning to come. Nice stuff, some of it.' I couldn't thank him for it; the words stuck in my throat, but there had been some long-distance bookings, and at this rate we would sail along and make a good profit. But nothing's for nothing.

'You scratch my back, I'll scratch yours. There's another little thing you can help me with.' He was almost laughing at me, expecting me to resist. 'Don't worry, boy. I want your professional advice, that's all. You're in the travel business, this is up your street.'

'The boys in the office will know more . . .'

'Not this. Now listen.' Suddenly it was all business. 'There's still a lot of perks in getting in illegal immigrants. I feel strongly about these boys, they're British same as us, aren't they? Pakistanis – Indians – we fought beside them in the Middle East, didn't we? And now we try to keep them out, poor bastards.'

He was at it again, whipping himself up into a state of belief before he pulled the trigger. I listened with half an ear to the pious stuff, then he explained, 'It's easy enough to get them on the planes that end. It's getting them off this end and past customs and immigration that causes trouble. There's been a lot of tightening up.

'Now all I want you to do is to tell me how to get airside

37

and back without using a pass at London's Heathrow Airport. Just a route to dodge the security boys to reach the aircraft.'

A quiet little bomb dropped right in my lap and was ticking merrily away while he watched me sweat.

'How can I know a thing like that?' I pleaded.

'You're in the business. Bloody well find out,' he shot back.

'But it's impossible. It can't be done. There'd be too many checks.'

'Balls,' he said and sat back leaving me with it.

He hid behind that middle distance stare of his. He used his unfocused gaze as a mask; it effectively hid his thoughts and gave him a sort of unhinged air of menace.

I should have got up and gone and taken the consequences. When I briefly considered what the consequences might be I wasn't sure that I was up to facing them. I pulled out the money and dropped it on the desk. 'Let's call it even,' I suggested.

His eyes flashed and thin hands gripped the desk as his lips drew back. 'Are you trying to insult me?'

'Christ! No. Look . . .'

'Then take that money back. I keep to my deals whether it's money or murder. You remember that, Spider. Now what's your problem?'

'You're asking me to nose around the airport to find a way of beating customs and immigration. If I was caught I'd be handed over to the fuzz and my agency's air licences would be taken away. It would finish me.'

'It'll finish you if you don't. You'll just have to be bloody careful, that's all.'

What had happened to friendly old Rex Reisen? This was a different man, the one I'd been expecting all along.

'I can't do it.'

'So you want to lose my business?'

'It makes no odds. I can be ruined either way.'

'I can pass the word round to the rest of the boys. They'll stop using you.'

'I know,' I said. 'It makes no difference.'

He had gone calm on me again and I knew that he'd have some little gem tucked away to try to intimidate me.

'Look, what are we quarrelling for? I respect you, Spider. I like a man who's not a yes-man. But someone's got to have control. Do you think I like putting on the pressure?'

He liked nothing more. 'Of course not,' I said. 'But,' I took him at his word, 'but, Rex, you must see where this can land me. It could ruin everything I work for.'

'What about what I work for? If you don't do it, Spider, then it could ruin my plans. So who holds most cards?'

'Surely there's another way.'

'Not as I see it. I want someone who has an excuse for being down there and can hold his tongue.'

'It's too risky for me. I've got to say no.'

I expected another outburst but he seemed to have discarded that line of approach. He sat back, his thin, nimble fingers manipulating another cigar into a firebrand. He looked me quizzically in the eye and his expression was soft but crafty. Just as I was wondering what dark alley his mind had dived down he started to tell me.

'Supposing Old Bill found your prints in the empty house?'

'They couldn't. I was too careful.'

'I said supposing.'

I didn't like this. 'They would tie me in with the report on Chapman.'

Reisen waved his cigar and grinned like a cat. 'Not only that but they might think you got him away. They wouldn't like that, Spider, with all the fuss about this geezer.'

'But I didn't leave my dabs.'

'No, you're too smart.' He rose, went to the drinks cabinet and fished around its illuminated gloss with a pair of ice tongs. 'Recognize this?' Between the tongs was a whisky glass. It did nothing to me. But I wondered why he was holding it so carefully.

'No,' I said. 'It doesn't turn me on.'

'It should. You had a drink out of it a few nights ago.'

The tongs reached my guts and stirred big chunks of ice around. 'So you pre-planned it just to hook me.'

'Don't be stupid. How can you pre-plan a thing like that? No. I just don't miss opportunities, Spider. I thought your dabs might come in useful one day. I didn't expect it so soon.'

'So what are you going to do with it?'

'Put it in the kitchen of the house then spread the word that the coppers missed something. They would be mad at the suggestion; madder still when they did a check; they would want blood, Spider – yours.'

'It wouldn't work.'

'With your form and your strange contacts you know bloody well that it would.'

And I did. I considered making a dive for the glass but he'd be prepared for that and his men were nearby. Anyway, he'd find another way of fixing me.

'I thought we were all palsy walsy?' I complained.

'But we are, my old mate.' He put back the glass but retained the tongs, doing a clever act of holding his cigar in them. 'I find it helps to have a little something on people in cases of emergency.'

We looked at each other while we assessed our relative positions. Master and slave. The ball and chain were invisible but were there just the same. My mind was racing round in tight circles probing how I could fix him and remain in one piece. Maybe the airport job wasn't so bad. 'I'll need some time to dig around my airline contacts,' I said.

'I know you will. To make sure that you don't stall I'm giving you two days. At the end of that time I'll send a driver and car to take you down to Heathrow.'

I could see that he was really enjoying his cigar; he was a long way from the old days when he shared a drag at a Woodbine behind somebody's broken fence.

On the way home I did a lot of work on the self-justification angle but at the end of it all I knew I was kidding myself. Reisen had hooked me for more than just casing the airport but at the moment I hadn't a glimmer of what it was about. If he was importing illegal immigrants for petty cash he wouldn't touch it himself or personally try to intimidate me. He was boss man of a rugged, vicious territory. So what was he at? Was he putting on a big act over Chapman? I was glad that Maggie was away. She was so honest herself that she would never understand how I became involved, but she would have winkled out of me that something was wrong.

I bought a paper and took it up to my room. My appetite had gone so I fixed myself a couple of eggs on toast and made a pot of coffee. Worried and lonely I sat with the television on without seeing any of it. There was no one to turn to in my sort of life, there rarely is. I didn't want any of the villains to know that Reisen had the clamps on me and it wasn't something I could tell to anyone on the right side of the law. My best friend was my younger brother but he was now a detective-constable and hardly the bloke to dump a problem like this on. Anyway, it was out of his manor. I was on my own, but I suppose a loner was my role.

One of the few things I boast about is the way I make coffee. I sat there enjoying my second big cup, knowing that nobody had taken Reisen on without finishing up dead and missing. I picked up the evening paper and started to read about the man who had inadvertently caused some of my current problems; it did not make me like him.

The Government had come up with a good one this time. With the inventive genius of politicians for misleading people, it always surprised me that they weren't all in the advertising game. They were trying to calm public opinion by saying that Alan Bruce Chapman had imparted very little to the Russians; that the ever-vigilant DI5, Fairfax and his mob, had cut off the supply almost before it began. The official line now was that a foreign power had sprung Chapman, hoping to squeeze out the valuable information that he carried around in his little overworked bonce. It sounded very good, for they went on to say that it was imperative to recapture Chapman. It sounded like a Fairfax special to me.

As I wasn't hopeful about Chapman's recapture, I used

the next two days picking the brains of some of the contacts I had with various airlines. It made me feel a bastard that under the guise of friendship I dug out some useful information about London's Heathrow Airport. I was amazed, too, at the ease with which the information came, but then they didn't know I was a villain; they took me on trust. The betrayal of that trust stuck in my gullet. I cursed Reisen but I knew what would happen if I didn't go ahead. I dug out every scrap of useful information that I could. Which was as well, because at ten o'clock bang on schedule Reisen's envoy called for me.

She was announced as Mrs Burns, which startled me because I had expected a man. As she entered my office I glimpsed Lulu giving her a quick, catty squint and could understand her envy. She wore smart blue slacks with buckled shoes peeping below them and a flared mid-calf military styled coat with a rakish yellow beret which suited both the long hair and her pert features. She had the slimness to carry the slacks. I had to admit that she looked almost edible and more relaxed than when I had first seen her in Reisen's office.

I didn't waste time asking her to sit down as I didn't want anything said in the office. Lulu, who seemed to disapprove of anyone who called for me, almost sniffed her contempt as I grasped Mrs Burns's elbow and gently propelled her out. My shares rose high with my staff as we went past the counter. She was undoubtedly an improvement on Knocker Roberts.

Outside, neatly parked on a meter, front wheels turned ready to go, was a sage-green E-Type. I had difficulty climbing in and didn't much like it with my legs stretched out in front of me. On the other hand, she looked just right and I could see why she had chosen slacks instead of a skirt.

We sat there to sort things out, so I said, 'I'm not going to call you Mrs Burns, so what's your first name?'

'Penny. You're direct, aren't you?'

'Not particularly; it just saves time. We're bound to come to it, anyway.'

She had a nice voice with just the lingering trace of a Scots accent. She still had that veiled look about her as if there was something that she did not want seen and was constantly on guard against. It was a trick of concealment that somehow mildly irritated me. She wore no rings but as she reached for the ignition I noticed a superb gold watch and bracelet that must have cost a bomb. Her clothes, too, reeked of expense and the crocodile handbag hadn't come from a jumble sale.

She created such an attractive, feminine picture that I had to remind myself that she was from Reisen. That was always good for destroying the mood and for making me behave myself. Her small hand went to the gear lever as one neat patent-leather-clad foot reached for the clutch pedal. She did all the right things and pulled slowly into the road with the powerful engine playing along with her. I was glad she was driving because it kept her gaze on the road and mine unrelentingly on her, in the subtle Spider Scott manner, of course. She slipped into the thick of the traffic and her lips twitched with amusement as she realized that I was watching her critically. In underworld circles it was considered that I could drive and she didn't seem put out by it. As we progressed I realized why – she was good with that singlemindedness that comes rarely in a woman.

'How on earth did Reisen collar you?' I asked her as we headed towards Knightsbridge in a series of slick but safe manoeuvres.

'You really are direct. I applied for the job. I'm a secretary – he needed one.'

Simple. How many secretaries had E-Types and solid gold bracelets on their watches? 'He pays well,' I observed.

'I earn it.' She did not elaborate.

'You know your way to the airport?'

'I've been before,' she rejoined.

'Picking up illegal immigrants?' I suggested, regretting it at once.

'You wouldn't want me to pass that back to Reisen, would you?'

'I couldn't stop you. But it doesn't answer the question. Let's not pretend you're working for charity.'

'To me he's no different from any other boss. I work regular hours and he pays well. In return I offer efficiency. Nothing more.' There was a mild emphasis on the last two words.

I let it drop, thinking I might have pushed it too far. She was defensive, which gave some clue. So we were silent for a bit while she grappled with traffic jams and bad drivers. Then she laughed and said, 'I wouldn't get many illegal immigrants in this, would I?' It broke the ice and I chuckled.

'The Reisen outfit seems to do all right,' I said. 'You with your E-Type and Knocker Roberts with his Aston Martin.'

'Now *there's* a car,' she said. 'That's what I'd like.'

Once when we stopped at traffic lights I noticed her gaze drifting to a fur shop across the way; it held her attention until we got a hoot from behind after the lights had changed.

'Furs interest you?' I observed.

'Don't they any girl?' And there was that quick defensiveness again suggesting that I should drop the subject.

When we reached the motorway I saw another of her facets. With the one-way lanes opening up before us she drove as if she herself was the power unit and the car was an extension of herself. She sat as if the bucket seat were custom-made to her very particular requirements. I didn't quibble when she easily smashed the speed limit because she wasn't careless. Speed was her metier and she constantly watched her mirrors for speed cops. Women drivers generally scare me silly but this one knew what she was doing; she wasn't putting on a show for me either.

Conversation died when she drove like this. I liked the way she held her head back showing a determined little chin and a good neckline. Her expression was one of relaxed concentration and for the moment I don't think I existed to her. And I wondered what else could turn her on and isolate her as she now was, self-contained, alive only to the moment.

She came to when we neared London Airport. Her eyelids fluttered as if she had broken a spell and she gave me a slightly embarrassed sideways glance as if she knew that I had caught her out.

'Welcome back,' I said, grinning.

She smiled briefly. 'Well, you men can't have it both ways. You accuse us of not concentrating and when we do you make snide comment.' The Scots side came through more strongly this time and sounded just right.

We were approaching the tunnel entrance to the airport and ahead I could see a VC10 standing on its tail as it took off, four black funnels of smoke unfurling into the ground like giant springs giving it extra push. At normal speed we turned in and Penny flipped on the sidelights as we got in a lane in the tunnel. 'Which building?' she asked.

'Number three. But you'll have to park. And I shall be working alone.'

She cut through the islands, past the taxis and illegally parked cars and pulled up behind an airline bus. 'You didn't think I was coming in with you, did you?' She was pleasantly winding me up.

'I wasn't sure. Reisen might have instructed you.'

She tossed her head as I climbed out and gave me an impish glare.

'I don't intend to break the law. That I must leave to you. When you're finished I'll be on top of Queen's Building or in the bar.'

That figured. She was the type to watch the big birds queueing up for take-off. I turned through the self-operating glass doors.

No 3 was the terminal for the really big birds who constantly crossed oceans until it was time to give them a brief medical before winging them away again. It had an aura that impregnated into the bloodstream and as a Sagittarian I was sensitive to it. Here and there the really hardened traveller, the country-a-day man, strolled by as if he was catching a bus, or hurrying because familiarity had made him cut it close.

45

I went up the stairs and crossed the bridge towards the administration block on the north side because I wanted to try an experiment. It is another dimension of life; a vast living community thrust together to get passengers and planes airborne; a freak rambling township that makes its own rules and lives differently from the rest of us. And behind the scenes they live, drink, breath aircraft and the only people who really understand them are in other airports throughout the world.

It was into this world of stiff collars and loosened ties, of offices and administration, of cargo lists and maintenance strike problems that I moved.

As I roamed these corridors I noticed that in the warm weather a good many doors were open and one or two rooms were empty. No one challenged me. I tried a couple of 'Good mornings' on people passing and was greeted back.

I wanted to be sure that there was no way down this side of the building to the aircraft side. I thought there might be a quick way out to the aircraft for the staff but there was not. So up here on the first floor they were bound the right side of customs and immigration. I must have traversed most of those corridors without hindrance until someone suspected I was floundering and asked if he could help and I said I was looking for Japan Airlines and he directed me. That's all there was to it; that and the fact that I saw a couple of dirty white overalls hanging up at the end of a corridor and nicked the larger pair. I had to find a way of avoiding police, customs, immigration, and airport security in order to reach the aircraft.

Back in the booking hall I had a cup of indifferent coffee to steady my nerves. Never before had I been stupid enough to try something completely illegal in front of so many witnesses. I noticed far more police than is usual here and worried about it until I remembered that all points of departure were being watched in case Chapman tried to slip through.

I went downstairs and approached the Pan American counter. To the left of it was a little gap, then the Air India

46

counter. It wasn't too difficult to hang around until the counter clerks of both airlines were busy handling baggage and tickets. There was a sprinkling of people around as I edged towards the gap between the counters.

Then I was through.

CHAPTER 4

Nobody shouted. Remembering what I'd learned, I entered an office immediately behind the Pan American counter, which oddly belonged to Air India. Shirt-sleeved Indians toiled away as I casually skirted their desks towards a door on the far side.

Some looked up in mild surprise but I did not hesitate. I was beyond the office before any form of real curiosity was aroused. Now I was in a concrete-floored corridor, but for a couple of clothes baskets, a bare no-man's-land of a place.

This was where the real danger lay; this would have to be the biggest bluff. As I turned right I noticed a couple of men talking together just a few feet to my left. One of them saw me but continued talking. Hands in pockets I sauntered on until I came to an opening on my left.

If there was to be a challenge then it must be here.

But there was no one there; just daylight at the end of a short tunnel. I moved towards the light and suddenly I was airside.

Spread out in front of me were several huge aircraft, some just arrived, some about to go. The passenger tunnels poked long fingers from the palm of the departure lounge towards aircraft hatches. The customs–immigration were all behind me. But I could still sense them so I moved farther along the side of the building.

There were too many people doing too many jobs to worry about me. Vans and jeeps roamed and I saw one of the London Airport Authority vans; red and mauve diagonal parallel runways painted vividly on its glossy side. That was what I had to beware of; the eternal scouting round the airport perimeter.

Out there in the sun floated the sleek bodies of the air giants, carrying their colours as proudly as jockeys in an important race. They held head and tail high as they lingered out of their element while being preened.

I had done what Reisen wanted of me and it was time to go.

I considered it too risky to return the way I had come. So I went round the side of the building towards the gates through which vehicles passed. Because I was once a creeper and have a sharp eye for danger I noticed odd bits of detail. Some of the vans, for instance, carried yellow labels with the black letters CT in their centre. I wondered what it meant.

At the right-hand side of the open double gates was a shelter for the guard who examined the passes. It would be difficult getting in that way, much too chancey. Then what about getting out?

He saw me coming but wasn't throwing a tantrum over it. I knew that the passes were about the same size and colour of my new red driving licence. The difference was inside; the passes carried your name and the company you worked for, together with a mug shot. Up to now I was just another returning bod and to show just how familiar I was with the routine I stuck doggedly to the middle of the road, which would keep him a little distance from me.

As I neared the gates the guard looked up, the sun catching his glasses and his uniform peak and I moved my hand towards my pocket where my driving licence was, intending to wave it to him. Just at the moment I was getting ready to run in case it went wrong he shot me a grin and waved me through. If this was the security I couldn't understand why the 'boys' kept the airport jobs down to a steady million a year.

I found Penny on top of Queen's Building, the wind rip-

48

pling her hair about her face. She was now wearing large tinted spectacles.

'Look at that.' She pointed to the planes queueing up to take off. 'I'd like a fleet of those,' she said. She didn't seem curious about where I had been.

'I managed to get out to the planes,' I said.

'I don't want to know.' She almost snapped and when I looked at her I could see that she had already removed it from her mind. We headed for the car park.

'I see. So you don't mind driving me down here to do a job but you don't want to know anything about it. Is that how you salve your conscience?'

'I don't know what you mean.' A plane roared off and she turned to watch it lift above the buildings.

'You like to pretend that if you don't know the details of a job you're off the hook. Ignorance is bliss.'

'I don't know why you're here. I was asked to bring you down, that's all.'

'Well, I don't want to hold out. I've been casing the airport to see if we can get those illegal immigrants in and out of the country.'

'Really! Well, keep it to yourself. I've no wish to know.'

'But you *do* know. I've just told you.'

'Then you must be joking. Here's the car.'

Her ostrich-like attitude astounded me. She was intelligent yet the only person she was kidding was herself. Was this how she lived with herself?

For the next twenty minutes we were silent and for some reason I was angry. I didn't believe in self-delusion. I reckoned that you should be able to look yourself right in the eye and call yourself a chiselling bastard if you behaved like one. When we reached the heavy traffic she relaxed again. She turned briefly to smile at me, and it was spontaneously warm. 'Have you time for a coffee?'

'I'll make time.'

She nodded, swung past a bus and skirted a taxi.

I don't know what I was expecting; but when she pulled up outside one of those mews cottages in Chelsea I was surprised. I climbed out onto the cobbles and thought how attractive it looked with all the front doors painted different colours, and flowers sprouting from their gay windowboxes to catch the sun.

'There's a row of garages round the back,' Penny explained as she opened up the centre primrose door. Inside, she took off her coat and beret, while I had a look around. The area was expensive and the cottage hadn't been bought with cigarette coupons either. It was discreetly but very expensively furnished with off-white, deep-pile, wall-to-wall carpeting and white leather armchairs. There was little that wouldn't appreciate in value, from the wall paintings to the antique porcelain figures in a Georgian cabinet. There was nothing flashy about any of it. It reeked quality. In the old days I would have enjoyed screwing a drum like this and would have got a good price for anything here that I might have nicked.

'You like it?' She had seen my appraisal.

'Very much. Good taste.'

'Thank you. I'm surprised that . . .' she tailed off, embarrassed.

I grinned and finished it for her. 'That someone like me can appreciate good things? That shouldn't really surprise you.'

'But you *were* a burglar and I know you've been to prison. I thought that the deprivation of liberty . . .'

'That's the very reason, isn't it? It's because I was a villain that I learned to admire good things. I had to in order to nick the right ones.' I wondered why she avoided criminal slang; working for Reisen she must know it as well as I did.

I continued looking around and said, 'I know a fence who would give me a fair return for some of this lot.'

'I dare say. Black or white?'

'Mmm? Oh, white please.' She was wearing a pure silk blouse, fine and transparent with gold filigree work over the breasts and down the arms. As she turned towards the kitchen I could see her white bra, and noted that her hips were the right size for slacks.

She brought back coffee on a Sheffield Plate tray which she set on a small Regency table.

Stirring in sugar I asked, 'Why do you kid yourself about what Reisen does?'

'He does have legitimate businesses,' she countered.

'But it doesn't change the man.'

She sipped her coffee and eyed me disconcertingly. 'Perhaps I'm a little ashamed of myself.'

'Why? Has he got something on you?'

She shot upright, spilling some of her coffee in the saucer. 'What a ridiculous idea.'

Then she said, relaxed again, 'Where can I find another job to provide me with this sort of living?'

'What did you do before?'

'I worked as a shop assistant in a Glasgow milliner's and learned shorthand and typing during the evenings. My mother's still there. My father was a policeman.'

'Was?'

'He was sent to prison for taking a bribe from a suspect.'

I shut up then. I could never stand bent coppers.

'Have I shocked you?' she prodded.

'Not really. It happens all the time. If there was another job to keep you like this, with a reputable company, would you take it?'

Penny smiled over her cup. 'What you're really asking is would I leave Reisen?'

'All right.'

'I tried it once; got a job in a staff agency. Reisen put on pressure in the right quarter and I was fired. He's very possessive. Now it would be difficult to leave.'

'Why? Do you know too much?'

'Don't be silly. I know nothing of Reisen's deals other than the legitimate ones. If the police *tortured* me they'd get nothing from me because I've got nothing to tell. Reisen is nobody's fool.'

'So you don't know why he's using me?'

'If I did I wouldn't tell you. But I've no idea. Please pass your cup.'

'What would you suggest I do?'

Penny laughed and it wiped away the barrier that was almost always there. 'Talk it over with your wife.'

'You know I haven't got one.'

'At your age?' She eyed me critically. 'Thirty-five? You should have. You're only ugly when you pry.'

'Where's your husband?' I countered.

I saw a flash of something; reminiscence; regret; it was difficult to tell but I had penetrated.

'I resolved not to re-marry a long time ago.'

In spite of her reticence, I thought I saw a way of getting information from her. I sent out a little silent prayer to Maggie for what I was about to do. But Maggie was reprieved, for something held me back and I nearly always heed those sort of warnings.

I couldn't slot Penny in. She had undoubted charm and femininity but there was the shuttered element that I couldn't reach. Finishing my coffee, I rose.

'Don't go. Not yet.'

I hesitated. She was quickly pouring herself another coffee.

'Sit down until I've finished this. Please.'

So I sat, listening to mild little warnings in my head.

She was agitated, slowly stirring her coffee like a drummer using the brushes. 'If Reisen offered you a job, would you accept it?'

'I've just done one for him.'

'I mean a real job.'

Suddenly, by implication, she was suggesting that she very much knew all about Reisen's other little enterprises.

'What sort of a job?' I countered.

'Don't be awkward. Say a snatch.'

She was looking at me disarmingly yet she had shut herself out again, as if her words were monitored. But at last she was speaking the right language.

'No. I wouldn't do it.'

'Why not?'

'I've never worked for mobs. I don't go for violence.'

'All right, then why did you go in to the airport today for him?'

'You know Reisen. He has his charming little ways.'

'Do you think then that after five years of working for him I have any way of escaping his charming little ways even if I thought I'd had enough?'

I was silent for a while. I had found it difficult enough with Reisen myself and had only just met him. Then I said, 'Is all this hypothetical? I mean, you're taking a chance with me, aren't you?'

'You're not like the rest. That's not an emotional answer, I just happen to know.'

'It would depend on how badly you wanted to leave him.'

She finished her coffee, putting down the cup wearily. She picked up the huge tinted glasses and put them back on as if they would change everything for her. 'I suppose it would.' She looked across and smiled. 'It's all talk, I suppose. But if the question seriously arose I know I'd need help.'

'You've done well, boy. That's a fact.'

Reisen was wearing a brown shirt today with a black tie, probably for someone he had just had removed. A sentimentalist, Reisen. I could afford to feel facetious; I was beginning to believe I was at last off the hook. Not that I believed he had levelled about the job but I wasn't inquisitive.

I started to rise but Reisen held up a restraining hand.

'Hold on, boy. Just a minute. Look, for a nice fee do you think you could do it just once more, and take someone with you?'

'Why not half a dozen?' I said sarcastically. 'They'll form a nice crocodile going past the Pan Am counter and through the Air India office.'

'No, I'm serious. I've got a Pakistani who's kicking up rough. I want to send him back. He'll get himself on the plane.'

I couldn't believe it. If Reisen had someone kicking up rough what was wrong with his usual remedy? 'Why don't you just buy him a ticket and send him back openly?'

Reisen was startled. Paying out for a real ticket had not occurred to him. 'He'd need a passport, wouldn't he?'

I was startled in return. Since when had Reisen been stumped by a little thing like a passport. What was he playing at? 'He'll need an embarkation card for getting aboard.'

Reisen hesitated as if uncertain but I wasn't fooled. He very well knew what I had told him.

'Perhaps you're right,' he agreed. 'Let's forget it. Look, you wouldn't want to come in on a job, would you, Spider? I can use your special talents.'

His approach was almost pathetic. 'I don't operate on mob snatches.'

'Who said it was a snatch?' He came back quickly.

'It's your style. OK? But it's not mine.'

He looked at me speculatively but he wasn't pressing, which worried me more than if he had been. I wished I understood one part of the crafty game he was playing. It was unlike Reisen to be conciliatory. Any bravado I showed was strictly for him; I wasn't kidding myself. Come to think of it, I wasn't kidding Reisen either.

'You wouldn't have to be in on the snatch itself. It's your driving ability and that knack you have of going to earth when it matters. You're the right bloke in an emergency, Spider boy.'

I was getting in deeper each time we met. It was all right taking a stand, but where would it get me? I didn't want to finish up like Ossie Jenkins. Even so, I heard myself saying, 'No thanks. I'm strictly a loner. I'm no organization man.' I must be mad to sound so emphatic.

I thought he was about to argue but suddenly he shrugged.

'Maybe you're right. Anyway, think it over, boy, and if you change your mind, let me know, eh!'

He offered me a drink, which I refused, and then he said, 'Do you know Spud Murphy's place?' Everyone knows Spud's place. He throws fantastic parties, kicks up a hell of a shindy in his top-floor suite of a modern block, yet strangely the neighbours never complain. Reisen went on, 'He's throwing a "do" tomorrow night. You could take Penny Burns along.'

'Perhaps she has other plans.'

He grinned. 'You're a good-looking boy, you know that? Tall and dark and willing.' Reisen laughed. 'How did you get on with her today?'

'She's a good driver.'

'Is that all?' He was enjoying himself at my expense. Then he pressed a desk button and Penny appeared at the door, ignoring me and looking inquiringly at Reisen.

'Spider wants to take you to Spud Murphy's tomorrow. He doesn't drink so you can let him do the driving.'

'Wait a minute.' I rose in embarrassment. 'You don't have to come. You're being forced into this.'

I heard Reisen laugh but focused on Penny.

'It's all right,' she said. 'I'd like to go with you. Really. Spud's parties are quite something. Can you pick me up at seven?'

'There you are,' roared Reisen. 'What were you worried about? OK, Penny. Wrap it up for the night.' And after she had gone, 'I tell you, boy, you don't want to underestimate yourself. She'll be very happy to go with you.'

It wasn't until I was outside that I realized what a clever little trap it had been. No one had asked me whether I wanted to go.

Half of London's underworld was there.

Reisen wasn't. There were odd offshoots from top society and some film starlets hanging on to a few of the boys. I could never understand the perverted sort of glory that some of these people got from mixing with villains. Some of the boys present were the toughest, roughest and completely unscrupulous villains in the game. It was in their blood, deep and clotted and there wasn't the slightest chance of remedy. It never seemed to get through to the actress types who might enjoy a bit of brutal love-making that boyfriend was likely to go straight out to cosh someone and perhaps make a cabbage of him for life. There were one or two coppers present, too. They would have been invited but whether they were bent or had come hopefully with big ears flapping I couldn't know.

From the way some of the waiters moved about it wouldn't have surprised me if the Flying Squad had planted some men among them, but they were wasting their time; there would be no confessions tonight and no planning. The boys were here to amuse themselves and judging by the raucous laughter they were doing just that.

I steered Penny through the smoke and chatter to the quietest corner and we grabbed some eats and a drink.

I noticed that she now wore a wedding ring. It was strange that she had never mentioned her husband and I wondered if she was widowed or divorced. She caught me eyeing the wide band of gold.

'Don't worry,' she said. 'It dates back to the dark ages. It's been over a long time.'

It didn't seem to worry her for she was clearly enjoying herself, her bright eyes sweeping up people with a child's interest, dissecting the women and financially bracketing them. There were faces I knew, a few I'd met doing bird. Considering the number of years a lot of these boys had spent behind bars it was not surprising that they enjoyed the recession. I'd spent nearly seven years doing porridge myself. Not again. Not ever. Reisen or no Reisen.

'A right bunch of villains,' I observed.

'Some of them are very amusing.'

'Why did you let Reisen bully you into coming with me?'

'I wanted to come with you. Why, is it a strain?'

'With you? You're joking. I wonder why he didn't come himself?'

She nudged me. 'Stop fishing, Spider. He does have honest interests, as I've said before.'

'Such as?'

'Oh. Building. Demolition. Restaurants. Estate Agents . . .'

'Estate Agencies?' I'd spoken too sharply for she looked up quickly, her gaze inquisitive.

'Why, does that surprise you?'

'It doesn't really. But I've been poking around for a place on and off. Which ones does he own? Maybe he can help me.'

'I can't think of their names offhand. I'll let you know.'

'Is A. Nole and Co one of them? I saw they had a place up for sale in the Kensington area which might interest me.' I was taking chances but I had to. She didn't appear suspicious as she replied, 'It seems to ring a bell. I can find out for you.'

Suddenly she slipped her arm through mine as someone pushed past. Afterwards she made no attempt to break away and I found her gentle pressure pleasantly disturbing. Then she looked up at me, gave me a tug and asked, 'Would you prefer to come to my place? I can scrape up a quick meal.' There was no other inference in her tone. 'You don't have to,' she added as I hesitated.

'Let's go,' I said.

In her mews cottage she poured herself a slug of whisky as if she had suddenly resolved to get tight and damn the consequences. She insisted that I drank with her, but I'm a great sipper. Slipping off her shoes she padded about in her stockinged feet and disappeared into the kitchen.

She produced grilled fillet with eggs and some potato croquettes. It was a queer sort of meal but enjoyable and Penny kept up an amusing chatter as though she hadn't talked for years and wanted to get it all off her chest. None of it concerned Reisen. Even though her hand reached more often for the whisky than the wine she did not become careless with her words.

'The coffee will be some time,' she finally said, with a silly sort of smile on her face. Then she whipped out some pins from her hair, letting it fall to her shoulders and shaking it out like a dog. 'Gives me a headache on top,' she said as if the drink had nothing to do with it. Then she came to stand over me and I could see that the devil was in her. I was looking up at her, half grinning, wondering what she would get up to next, when she promptly sat on my lap and clasped

57

her hands behind my neck. I didn't feel like pushing her off either.

'Am I too heavy for you?' She smiled down at me. As if it mattered. She slowly stroked one side of my face and I made a big effort to break away somehow without managing to move a muscle. The next moment she was kissing me slowly and expertly and I was thinking that you only live once so helped her along as best I could.

When she pulled away it was only fractionally, her lips almost touching mine, and I found myself looking into big hazel eyes. Her soft arms were about me, and I wasn't complaining about the rest of her either.

'You can help me, Spider.' She really breathed the words against my mouth. But I wasn't that gone. 'What with?' I breathed back.

'You can help me break with Reisen. It's not easy but it can be done. If you help.'

'Why not?' I said recklessly. 'I'll fix the punk.' That was Spider Scott the great hero. Spider Scott the great lover took over and was greeted with a great deal of warm, prolonged passion. It wasn't my fault she had drunk so much.

I finished making the coffee myself, strong, black and hot; I needed its strength and Penny just needed it. I handed it to her along with a hairpin that had fallen out. She was still bright, no resentment or regrets, but a little shutter had fallen down and I wondered if she was worried about speaking too much.

'Look,' I said. 'Don't worry about what you said about Reisen. We all get fed up with our jobs from time to time.'

She smiled briefly. 'Oh, Reisen's all right. At least he doesn't try it on. Take no notice of me. Anyway, I wouldn't want to land you in a spot.'

'What about coming house hunting with me on Saturday? Find out if that estate agent is one of Reisen's, then if they have what I want we might swing a deal.'

I pulled her up and she kissed me lightly on the cheek.

'Thanks for the evening, Spider. Don't think too badly of me. I may earn money but I lead a pretty lonely life.'

That could be true. Only an idiot like me would fool around with Reisen's secretary.

We livened up the wrong end of Kensington in the E-type with me driving. Apparently A. Nole and Co did belong to Reisen, which made the whole business stink. Going with her openly like this meant that if she did tell Reisen I at least hadn't tried to hide it. I was *genuinely* looking for a place. Also, if the agent knew Reisen I would be very surprised if he didn't know Penny or at least of her; so he was unlikely to report back.

I gave the agent my name and introduced Penny and saw a quick flash of enlightenment cross his heavy features. We all sat down at his desk while I told him what I was looking for. He produced photographs, figures and trotted out the old spiel about this place and that. He was good, too; not overdoing it, his watchful eyes behind the black-rimmed specs reaching right out into my bank balance. He was a good judge, which was why he became half-hearted.

After beating about the bush and noting that Penny was almost as bored as the agent of the type of property I was considering, I said, 'What about that place in Arbroath Road?'

'What place?'

'On the corner of Arbroath and Cecil. You've got a sign up.'

'Oh, that place. It's sold.'

'What is the sign still up for then?'

'I think you'll find there's a Sold sticker across the board.'

'So it's definitely not for sale?'

'Not unless the deal falls through.'

'Would you let me know if it does?'

'Sure. You're wasting your time though.'

'Can I have a look round it meanwhile?'

'The keys are with the buyer. It wouldn't be right, any-way.'

He was beginning to dislike me but I had a good start on him.

Finally I was glad to get out. Penny had been getting impatient at my prolonged searching and because I hadn't been digging around property in Mayfair. Later that day, alone, I returned to the house in Arbroath Road. There was practically no chance of the police watching it. Mr Alan Bruce Chapman was hardly likely to return. There was no sticker across the notice which still proclaimed it for sale.

Something bloody funny was going on and I felt as if I were in the centre of it. I began to argue with myself, but how can you argue with your own nature? I needed my head examined, I knew it. Just as equally I knew that I was going back into the house that night.

CHAPTER 5

If I was quiet the last time then this time I was a ghost. I went in the same way as before because I knew it to be quick and safe, but I left the window open from the outset. To test a theory I went down to the front door. It was bolted from the inside again. Well, well. It came as no surprise to find the back door bolted, so I crept back up to the first landing.

Crouching, I eyed the stairs leading to the next floor. I was straining so much for sound that if a feather fluttered to the floorboards I would have heard it. I started on up the last flight and waited outside the room where the camp bed had been. Very slowly I turned the handle. I inched that door open, fervently hoping that the hinges wouldn't creak. When I was able to squeeze through I waited and listened. It was barely audible but to an old creeper like me it was as good as a whistling kettle; the sound of slow regular breathing. I slipped in and left the door ajar.

There was a dim greyness near the window but the rest of the room was black. Testing each floorboard, I homed on to the sound of breathing. It was a long route keeping to the walls and I had to crouch past the window but there was far less risk of a creaking board.

The breathing was lower down than I expected and then I realized that it was coming from floorboard level. When I finally saw the dark shadow of the blanketed form with its pale circle of face, I was almost on it. Without moving my feet, I crouched to peer closer. He was sleeping so steadily that he might have been drugged. Shaking him gently, I shone my torch into his face.

I was prepared for a reaction but not for what followed. He shot up in his sleeping bag like a jack-in-a-box, eyes staring wide into the torch beam, terror on his face. Then the torch was spiralling across the room like a distant lighthouse gone mad and he sprang from his bed, lunging as he came. It was a wild blow and didn't hurt but it knocked me back on my heels while he ran for the door. He didn't notice it was open and ran into it. He cursed and moved just as I hurled myself in a tackle at his ankles. Sagging against the now closed door, he struggled like a maniac.

Even in the heat of it all I was very conscious of the noise and the fact that the torch had come to rest with its beam directed at the window wall.

'I don't intend to harm you,' I flung at him as he got one bare foot loose and started kicking at my face. How could he believe me when I was hanging on to him like grim death? His action was frantic; there was no science in it but he aimed such a rain of blows at my head that I had to release him to put up my arms to protect myself.

Finding himself free he snatched at the door but I shifted my body against it. His blows were becoming feebler and I heard a sob. He was half demented. Trying to climb to my feet I underestimated him as he went berserk on me again, but I found it easier to cover up as the sting faded from his blows. When he tried to scratch my face with his nails I ducked and thumped him one in the guts. I knew that he'd been scared out of his wits but there was a limit to what I was prepared to take.

Doubling up in front of me he held his stomach and retched. I was breathing like a cart-horse out with the hounds on a frosty morning and we made an odd pair in that darkened room. As it was we must have created such a din that I expected the neighbours to grab their phones.

Guiding him back to his bedding, I said, 'I'm not here to harm you or turn you in. Now relax.' Pushing him on to his sleeping bag, I took a quick, oblique look through the window. No neighbouring lights had come on, thank God, but it was still dicey. Grabbing the torch I snapped it out just as I saw his head come up and cunning creep into his eyes as they focused on the door.

'Not again,' I warned. 'If you want the fuzz here you just kick up another shindy like the last. Don't be a bigger bloody fool than you've already been.'

I think I got through to him. In case I hadn't I crouched in front of him with the door behind me.

'What do you want?' he mumbled. It was pitiful; the truculent demand of a renegade schoolboy. I gazed at the hunched shadow that was Alan Bruce Chapman and thought that there wasn't much of him. His outline was slight. All I could see of his face were the two pale blobs of his eyes. He held his head back as if afraid to lower it in case it fell off. And it was cocked at a slight angle as though listening to distant sounds. He had to be clever to hold down the job he'd had, but how had they misjudged the strength of his character so badly? How do such men get through?

Yet even in the darkness I could feel a kind of depth to the man but then I'm a low-born loner with nothing to guide him but sheer animal instinct – and a little hard experience. But I was glad not to be weighed with *his* complexes – I had enough of my own.

I tried to make out what I could of that thin figure in the gloom. Was he a man of great strength to have divulged secrets as he had or was he just another bloody weakling who had passed the security checks? Right now he was a frightened man and I felt a tinge of pity; I knew what it was like to be hunted.

'I don't know what to do about this,' I mused.

His head came up slowly and long fingers covered his face.

'I should have thought it abundantly clear.' There was a great weariness in his voice as though he'd decided it was all over. As I knew I couldn't stand another stretch of bird myself I was emotionally involved with this character who faced a thirty-year stretch or more. I loathed him for being a traitor, for placing us all in jeopardy, but I had the greatest sympathy for him in what he had to face. I'm too soft for a villain.

'Who's looking after you?' I asked.

'I don't know.' Then as he sensed my antagonism, 'I *really* don't know. I haven't the slightest idea who arranged my escape. I was brought here and food and drink is fetched in by people ostensibly viewing the house. They leave it downstairs for me to collect later. I bolt the doors at night and unbolt them in the morning.'

'Then who gives you your orders?'

'I don't know her name.'

'Her? A woman? What does she look like?'

'I've only seen her twice. The second time she looked quite different. Different wig, make-up, clothes ...' His voice was becoming stronger.

'Yet you knew it was the same woman?'

'Oh yes. The voice was the same and she couldn't change the bone structure of her face. She was clearly satisfied to confuse me over her appearance so that I'd have difficulty identifying her if it came to the point.'

'Young or old?'

I think he smiled in the gloom. 'I'd say she was young, but then she did change a decade or so between appearances.'

'So what happened the night I called?'

'I was unaware that you had. Do you mean when two men with stockinged faces broke in at about three in the morning, took me to an old farmhouse some miles out of London and then brought me back in the middle of the night twenty-four hours later?'

'But you weren't here when I called before that time.'

'Oh, I see. I was told to stay in the attic that night.'

I couldn't make sense of it. 'Do you know a man called Reisen?'

He thought a bit. 'You mean the gangster?' And when I nodded, he added, 'No, of course not. I'm unlikely to meet such people.'

'For a bloke who's been mixing with Russian spies you've got a queer slant on yourself.'

'Look here,' he said, 'where is all this leading? You obviously know who I am, who are you?'

'It's much better that you don't know. What I can't make out is why you're just content to sit here and take orders from a girl.'

'Can you suggest an alternative?' As he realized he had nothing to fear from me his voice changed to an authoritative tone. He was now talking down to me although not consciously.

'Then what are they going to do with you?'

From the way his head jerked back I could see that he hadn't liked the way I'd phrased it. A tinge of fear was back in his voice when he replied, 'Get me out of the country.'

I let it hang and when the silence became awkward, slipped in, 'Aren't you afraid? I mean, how do you know they're not going to knock you off?'

It wasn't cold but he huddled into himself and swayed very slightly from side to side. 'That's the least of my worries; the idea of death doesn't bother me. For me to die would perhaps be the best answer for us all. But I can't do it myself.'

I respected him for that. 'Then why are you so afraid?'

Wearily he unclasped himself only to draw his knees up under his chin. 'Prison appals me. To mix with those men and their habits— But what really terrifies me is the possibility of being sent to Russia.'

This man was levelling all along the line. I had been

listening for the lies, deceit, but there were none. If he was like this in court he'd crucify himself. 'Why the hell did you do it?'

'Does it matter?'

'It matters to me. I've got to make up my mind what I'm going to do about you.'

'I'm guilty, if that's what you want.'

'That's obvious or you'd take your chance in court. Stop stalling.'

'There's a limit to what I'm willing to tell you, whoever you are. You're obviously not the police. I'll say this much; I was deliberately careless.'

'Who are you kidding? Why do it at all then?'

'I had to do it to appease the Russians. They had precious little out of me, though, and to insure I didn't give more I saw to it that I was caught.'

Crouched as I was my legs were aching so I took a chance on chummy and squatted on the deck. I had wondered why he was being so open but I supposed that he was almost beyond caring. What difference could it make to him? After the earlier scare I think he was glad to talk, even to a stranger who had dropped in during the middle of the night.

'And now you don't know who sprung you but you're hoping it's not the Russians; if it is they'll take you back to the fabulous free city and put your head in a squeezer until it's dry of what it holds. Is that it?'

'It's not exactly how I would phrase it but that's about it. I really can't see myself resisting the sort of pressure they're likely to apply. I'm not the stuff heroes are made of.'

I was beginning to wonder. A man who had sent himself to the wall and wasn't afraid to die had something in him. The pressure the KGB had applied couldn't have been a direct threat to himself but to someone else, otherwise I reckoned he would have told them to get stuffed. They couldn't know that he had virtually given himself up, which was as well for whoever he was protecting.

'So why not give yourself up and tell them in court?'

65

He laughed drily. 'Don't you see? My motive is the one thing I must conceal in order . . .'

'To protect someone else. It has to be a bird,' I said. He didn't reply.

Then he said, 'I'm sorry to burden you with this. You're just a friendly voice in the dark. I haven't talked about it before but my head's been bursting with it.'

'You won't go that extra bit and tell me about it?'

'I'm sorry; I can't. Not to anyone.'

I felt that he had a pretty soul-destroying story to tell. God! Look at the state of him; from high office to a scared scarecrow; from comfort to bare boards. I felt choked, particularly as I couldn't leave it like this.

We sat like a couple of dummies in what must have been a bizarre scene; a bare room in an empty house and two men squatting in total darkness. All the time I was stalling, wondering what to do about chummy. I think he realized it for he suddenly said, 'If you can't say who you are, at least tell me *what* you are.'

'Oh, I'm a creeper, a burglar.'

'Robbing an empty house?' I could hear his disbelief.

'I always find them easier. We all have to learn somewhere.'

'It's surprising, isn't it,' he observed at a tangent, 'what one can learn of people without seeing their faces. Here we are, two disembodied voices conversing for the first time together. Already you know my fears. For my part, I can feel your strength; I wish to God I had it.'

'Strength?' I was surprised.

'Not physical, though you have that too.'

'Can't you find out who's behind this?'

'I've been told to stay here when I hear someone arrive.'

'And you take notice? Why don't you do a bunk?'

'Where would I go? I don't have the experience I suspect you have of being on the run. What are we going to do? Are you going to tell the police?'

'There's no chance of that,' I assured him. 'I couldn't grass to a copper even if I despise what you've done. The

66

best thing we can do is to pretend we never met. You don't grass about me and I won't grass about you. OK?'

He thought about it and finally concluded that he had no choice. To tell his allies about my visit might create a panic move on their part that could result in disaster. If he didn't trust me there was little he could do about it; he had nowhere to run. Reluctantly he agreed. 'I give you my word.' Again there was emptiness in his tone suggesting that he was resigned to almost anything. His life had somersaulted; he was content to drift with whoever cropped up.

'Good. Well, I'll pop in again. Bit of company. I'll knock on the door next time. Three shorts and a thump. OK?'

Taking a last long look at his hunched shadow I said quietly, 'Cheer up, mate.' I wanted to tell him that prison wasn't so bad but he'd levelled with me and I couldn't lie to him about a thing like that. 'Is there anything I can bring you?'

He looked up. 'Are you really going to come back?'

'Why not?'

'Then I'd like some boiled sweets. They refuse me cigarettes here which of course does make sense. A match flare or smoke might be seen.'

'I'll bring you some. Get some kip now.' As I left the room I somehow did not think that he would.

Back at my digs I hooked out the *Standard* and took a long look at A.B.C.'s mug shot. It was a stock photograph from the press files and showed a thin ascetic face with bright intelligent eyes. He had looked the camera in the eye with the assuredness of a successful man and held his head back and slightly to one side as I had seen in silhouette. Confidence and a trace of smugness flowed quietly from him, so it had obviously been taken before his problems began. There was no particular weakness in the face; the chin was a bit pointed but there was a direct firmness in his gaze. So what had reduced him to a shambles? His future was bleak. He hadn't much to look forward to.

While he was awaiting trial behind bars it must have struck him hard just what it was going to be like; he must have realized too that on remand he was seeing the soft side of jail. Which was why, having been sprung, he did not now want to return to nick. Oh yes, I could understand that all right. No one knows what doing bird is like unless they've tried it. And it's always worse than you think it's going to be.

Lying on my bed I jacked up some sympathy for A.B.C. because whichever way you look at it his life was over right now. Yet I'd have to shop him. The feeling made me sick. But what was I supposed to do? Let the Russians wring him dry? I couldn't tell the police for two reasons. Reisen had too many bent coppers on his books and it would leak back to him. And I couldn't grass to a copper, not even under hypnosis. So I'd have to do it some other way.

One thing was clear; Reisen was in it up to his rotten neck. This worried me. I just couldn't see Reisen springing anybody for the Russians; his patriotic ramble was for real. So what was going on and what the hell was he using me for?

At dawn I bathed and shaved, cooked a breakfast and went to the office very early, where one by one I gave the staff a dressing down for being late in. Once satisfied that they were dutifully ashamed and should follow my example, I let them get on with it and went back to bed.

About midday I awoke and rang Ray Lynch who had moved over to the *Sketch*.

'Hello, boyo,' his voice boomed at me. 'How's it? How's Maggie?'

He sounded sober and I believed he'd eased up on the bottle since he'd been given his by-line following the scoop over the Chinese business. 'She's on a cruise. She's fine. How's Sally?' I asked.

'I was going to ring you, boyo. We're getting married. Thought you might operate as best man for us.' He laughed and it was good to hear from Ray. 'You could do a bit of creeping and drum up a few wedding presents for us.'

'Congratulations, Ray. Give me the date later. Now I want some gen from you.'

68

'I didn't think you were ringing to say hello. What's it about?'

'Alan Bruce Chapman.'

'Christ! Don't tell me you're up to it again.'

'I'm not, but if I am I'll want ten per cent commission on the story this time.' That got him. So far as Ray was concerned the sun shone from my jemmy.

'Do you know anything about his family? Close associates? Is he married?'

'He's married to a lush, boyo. Worse than I was and that's saying something. I believe she's a bit of a nympho, too. I know the Old Man's been worried about her. I think they've been trying to get her in hospital for a bit of surreptitious treatment.' By 'Old Man', he meant the Prime Minister.

'Does he dote on her?'

'How the hell should I know? Men do stupid things over women. And vice versa. What's going on, old boyo? You got a line?'

'No. I was sitting here looking at A.B.C.'s photo and working up some theories.' However much I denied it, he would never believe I wasn't operating for DI5. To play along, I added, 'If you come up with any odd titbits, rumours, family trouble, that sort of thing, let me know, will you, Ray?'

'Of course, boyo. You know bloody fine I will. I'll dig around.'

'And, Ray. Keep it to yourself, matey. You know, not a word.'

That got him; the secret's between you and me touch. By the time we finished I think he reckoned that he'd been co-opted by the department.

Then I rang Fairfax and got the unobtainable. As that was one number I was never likely to forget I rang again and got the same result. When I checked with the telephone engineers they told me the number had been discontinued. Blast the man. The foxy old bastard trusted no one. If he'd wanted me to have his new number he would have told me. Well, there were other ways. I took a quick drive in the eleven hundred to Eaton Terrace in Belgravia, wasted fifteen minutes circling for a parking place, then walked back.

A maid answered the door all white pinafore and cap. She wasn't bad so I gave her a smile that made her retreat, and said, 'Hello, love. I would like to see Fairf— er, Sir Stuart Halliman.'

She had made up her mind that I didn't belong and had there been a tradesmen's entrance would have whistled me round to it.

'He doesn't live here.'

'Don't give me that. Tell him Spider is here in the flesh.' My reassuring smile made her nervous.

She stared uncertainly at me, then asked me to wait and closed the door in my face as if I'd come to pinch the silver; and it would be worth nicking, too. The door opened again and an elderly elegant woman stood there, all silks and diamonds with an emerald or two. She had no looks but was well-preserved like quality jam. She ladled some out now with a fruity voice as she looked down her nose at me.

'Sir Stuart moved from here some months ago. If you are a friend of his I imagine he would have told you.' How bitchy can you get?

Nevertheless, I maintained my devastating smile. 'Did he leave a forwarding address?'

'If he did I could hardly pass it on to a total stranger.'

'But did he, ma'am?'

'No, he did not.' And I was left facing the blank door again. Maybe she wasn't such a lady. I'd called Fairfax a few things in my time; now I thought of a few more. Just when I needed him most he had opted out on me.

I'd never felt so frustrated. Fairfax was the one bloke who would know how to play it clever and he'd gone to earth. But then he'd always had the knack of getting under my skin.

I tried to ring Penny, but getting through to any of Reisen's switchboards was worse than raising Prince Philip at Buck House. Finally I went round to her mews place and was about to slip a note through her door when my practised eye glanced at the lock. For a top villain's secretary it was disgraceful. Perhaps she relied on the underworld knowing of her billet and not being stupid enough to screw the drum of anyone on Reisen's payroll. It took me just a little longer than that thought to open the lock and slip in. As the opposite side of the mews comprised a blank wall there was a good chance I hadn't been seen forcing the lock.

Upstairs in the bedroom doorway I scanned the room methodically. It was an entirely feminine room, pastel shades and gilt and ivory coloured furniture. I walked over and examined the dressing table without taking my hands out of my pockets. Arden and Estée Lauder cosmetics. Perfume by Guerlain. A roll of the finest face tissues. And not a speck of powder on the glass-covered top. That meant a daily help. The place was too spotless for a girl who had to dash off to the office.

I had been in the bedroom before, of course, but my casing had been restricted to the bed area. There was a floor-to-ceiling white wardrobe with sliding doors. There was a great deal of character here – and money. Taking my time I tried to tune in to its mood, for it was mood and character I was searching for. I learned a good deal but wasn't sure whether I interpreted the many signposts right.

Back at the front door I wrote a note asking Penny to ring me that night, slipped outside into the mews, closed the door, was just about to slip the note through the letter box when Penny asked from just behind me, 'What the devil are you doing?'

'Oh! Hello.' Casual Spider. 'I was just about to put this through.' I held up the note, not sure whether she'd seen me close the door or not. And as I turned my head more fully towards her she was playing it very poker-faced.

'I thought you were trying to break in,' she said.

'Break in?' I turned to the lock. 'Blimey, if I was trying to break in I wouldn't need the note. Here, you may as well have it.'

She took it from me, read it, and her face relaxed. She was either acting well or I had just pipped her at the door.

'Look, I'll show you what I could have done,' I said, pulling out my magic mica and opening the Yale lock. 'After you.'

It didn't worry her; after all, she knew that I was a creeper. She flicked her gloves at my face as she went past, so I knew then that it was all right and followed her in.

'Reisen given you the afternoon off?'

'No, I'm having an extended lunch hour. Coffee?' I took her coat and she slipped out of her shoes but kept on a green beret.

Following her into the kitchen I said, 'You ought to get an external draught excluder down the edge of your front door and a better lock. It's too easy to open.'

She put on the percolator and waited for it to pop. 'Not when I'm indoors it's not. And when I'm not here it has protection.'

I wasn't sure what she meant but didn't want to make an obvious probe. Standing behind her, I slipped my arms round her, linking my fingers in front. She tilted her head back happily and I kissed her. Her hand came up behind my neck and she gently pressured my head down. It was better than being back at the office.

While we were drinking coffee in the drawing-room, and munching cold chicken, I said, 'Apart from anything else what made you think you could ditch Reisen? Those sort of salaries don't come easily.'

She was nibbling at a bone, eyeing me impishly over it. When I first met her mention of Reisen would have put up the shutters. 'I've some put by,' she said, still nibbling.

'Enough?' I glanced obviously round the room.

She wiped her fingers on a napkin. 'There's never enough. But I could be comfortable for a few years.'

'So?'

She shrugged, a lot of expression going into it. 'I haven't played fair with you, Willie. I didn't know you well enough at first. It was childish of me to pretend that I don't know what Reisen is. It's not easy to give up what he pays me, even for self-respect. I'm true to myself. That's important, isn't it? I'm not one of these hypocritical bitches who hand out their favours on committees as if they're God-given to save the poor as long as the poor stay poor.'

Now the odd thing was that although she was opening up quite vehemently, sitting there with her back straight and her head at a defiant angle, I still felt she was being guarded. I looked straight into those immensely attractive hazel eyes which didn't give a damn whether I believed her or not and momentarily it was as if I did not know her at all.

'You still doubt me, don't you? You've too honest a face for a villain.'

'That's been said before,' I grinned. 'No, I don't doubt you, Penny. I think you've got yourself into a fix and don't know how to get out.'

She said, 'Perhaps I'm developing a late conscience; perhaps I'm getting too near to things I'd rather not know about. I've worked for him so long now he's getting careless in front of me.'

'Careless enough for him to want to tuck you away if you tried to leave him?'

She looked at me a little uncertainly and moved her plate away. 'That would depend on how *he* looked at it. I'm not carrying positive evidence around. It's more that he's making odd comments to others in front of me about what he *might* be going to do. Just snatches which I'd rather not hear.'

'Such as?'

She probed her mind and wrinkled her nose in silent exasperation.

'Don't tell me if you'd rather not,' I said craftily.

'Oh, don't be silly. I know your reputation about grassing.' She eyed me earnestly and added, 'It's easy to believe, anyway.'

'Tell me what you think of Reisen – as a boss.'

'He's a good boss but he's so basically unsure that he has to assert himself in the only way he knows how; by terror.'

'So it's no use going to him with a friendly tale that you want to leave and look after your sick old mother.'

'He would immediately feel insecure and search for a remedy. And his remedies form a limited and well-tried formula. No, he wouldn't fall for that, Willie; he's far too good a psychologist. For such a crude man he has amazing insight into people. That, coupled with his first rule of life, "If in doubt, snuff 'em out," makes him very formidable indeed.'

'So you're in for keeps.'

Penny fell silent but it was the sort of positive silence that somehow indicated she didn't entirely agree. She was made of strong stuff but I didn't think she'd be reckless.

'What sort of things have you been overhearing?'

She smiled a little bitterly. 'There have been odd comments about an airport snatch.' She talked some more about it but came up with nothing definite; only the feeling that there was something big in the air, something with a nasty smell.

When we left nothing had been resolved but I felt that she was working on it, and that she would tell me if matters ever reached a point of maturity. As she walked out of view, a slim, elegant figure with a supple grace, it was impossible to imagine that she could ever know of Reisen, let alone work for him.

I wasn't interested in snatches at London Airport but I was interested in Alan Bruce Chapman because it would stick in my gullet until I did something about it. The Spiders of this world never learn. It wasn't Reisen who was mixed up and needed a psychiatrist; it was me.

I rang Reisen to tell him I had changed my mind about coming in on a job, that I would accept.

CHAPTER 6

We made an appointment for that evening at the usual place. Back at the office I hung around. An enterprising police photographer could get the scoop of his life with the number of villains who marched in and out of my shop. Lulu started to beef that she needed another girl to help her with typing. She was such a good little worker that I knew it to be true and rang up the agencies. I went home on the latish side and saw two broad backs on my way up the stairs to my room.

Coppers. If they gold-plated them I'd still know. It is not that I dislike them, my only real hate is drug pushers, but I am eternally wary of them. They were waiting outside my door like weather men; one with a homburg, the other hatless, both wearing light raincoats. I approached warily and they turned to face me. They knew who I was but they went through the routine.

'Mr Scott?' This from the elder.

'You know it.'

'May we have a word with you, sir? I'm Detective Chief Superintendent Newbound from Scotland Yard – Special Branch.' He held out his card, which I read with care because it gave me time to think. The craggy face on the photo was quite a good likeness. The other was much younger and darker and I assessed him as a sergeant.

'Come in,' I invited with the enthusiasm I reserved for coppers. I did my usual trick of grabbing my favourite chair before inviting them to sit down, which left the bed or a battered old armchair with one arm loose and the springs pushing through the seat like tank traps.

But the Superintendent was an old hand. He remained standing, which gave him a psychological advantage, and he smiled down at me quietly.

'What can I do for you?' I asked. Already he had forced me to speak so I thought, Special Branch! the crafty coppers allied to Fairfax.

'We wondered if you could tell us why you rang a certain number earlier today?'

'Which number?' How could they know? It had been unobtainable.

'930 0932.'

Then I remembered that I had called the operator to check for me and she had wanted my number to ring back.

'It's my favourite number,' I said. 'There's something about it that gets me. You know how it is.'

'It was the number assigned to Sir Stuart Halliman – before it was changed.'

'Get away! I wonder if he'd do a swop?'

The sergeant was looking at me with acute distaste. His dark brows converged over his sharp eyes and I could see he was longing to pin one on me. On the other hand, Chief Superintendent Newbound was amused. 'Come off it, Spider,' he said. 'We know you used the number before.' His face split into a tolerant grin. 'Why do you think it was changed?'

That was under the belt and it hurt. 'Leave me alone, fellers. I've done nothing wrong and if I want to dial a number then I'll just dial a number, OK?'

'OK. But you rang up for a purpose. Now we're at your disposal. What can we do to help?'

'If you know anything about me at all you know that I don't speak to coppers.'

Newbound chuckled. 'I'd been warned you were an awkward blighter. We're a special kind of copper, Spider. You must admit that.'

'Coppers are coppers,' I said.

Newbound turned to his oppo and then said conversationally to me, 'This is Detective Sergeant Chittle, by the way.'

'Poor feller. Can you let yourselves out?'

'You don't ring that number unless you have something very special to say.'

I said nothing.

'For God's sake grow up. Now what's it all about?'

'Look,' I said heavily. 'I'll speak to Fairfax or nobody. If he can't be bothered to contact me then he can get stuffed. And that means you as well.'

'We're representing Fairfax.'

'Like hell you are. I can see him sending the Special Branch round.'

'Come on, Sergeant, we're wasting our time. There's none so blind as those who won't see.'

'Buzz off,' I said.

At the door the Super turned round. 'You're acting just like a villain. Perhaps you haven't retired from creeping, after all.'

I gave him the soldier's salute and he shook me by giving a much more expressive one back. I could get to like him but he was still a copper and I've never spilled to one in my life. He was right, though. I still *behaved* like a villain.

I was at Reisen's place bang on time. The fact that I had joined the club hadn't reached his torpedoes at the first landing; they frisked me down like American actors playing gangsters on the big screen and I was shown into reception. The only change was the newspapers. This time Reisen came out to usher me into his office himself. He shook hands with me as if we'd both joined a secret society and our fingers slid apart.

Reisen had changed. It was true that he still smoked a sausage-sized cigar but everything else was different. He was dressed very quietly in a brown tweed with a perforated suede tie that suited him. A pale edge of beige silk discreetly crept from his breast pocket. His white silk cuffs protruded just the right amount. His face, too, was more serious, his expression cautious but hard. The flash and bounce had disappeared and this had a disquieting effect on me. I thought to myself that this is the real Reisen, if there was such a

77

thing. His quiet attitude conveyed that the playing was over; this was for real. He was serious enough not to offer me a smoke or a drink.

'I'm glad you decided to join us, Spider. It'll be a change to have a bit of class about the place. A real pro.'

I watched him warily in the knowledge that somehow the whole thing had been engineered so that I should join him. Again the feeling of being manipulated was very strong. When I had these feelings it didn't seem to matter which course I took; I still landed in it.

'What's the job?' I asked reasonably.

He thought a bit, then said quietly, 'Your part is largely casing. You're a master at it, that's why you made such a good loner. But don't be disappointed, Spider, boy; there's a part in the operation too.'

I noticed that of all the differences in him the most remarkable was in his eyes. They weren't soft and doglike any more but had an emptiness that brasses who have been too long on the game possess; a sort of dark hopelessness that recognizes itself but is too far gone for anything to be done about it. I began to feel afraid of him.

'It's an airport snatch,' Reisen went on. 'They're keyed up on raids on the cargo sheds, so I've come to the view that it's best to hit when the stuff is in a van or on its way to the plane.'

'Which airline?' It was too late for my heart to sink; its weight was anchoring me to the chair. Suddenly I wanted to get out.

'We're not sure yet, boy. Probably Pan Am. We're waiting to hear from stateside.'

I noticed that he hadn't mentioned the cargo. 'Why there if it's leaving from here?'

'An advice note is sent over there; it's that end where our adviser is.'

'And what sort of casing do you want me to do?' I hoped I sounded interested.

'Heathrow Airport. But not the soft job you did before. This has got to be a thorough job – the McCoy.'

'I thought the last one was.'

'It was great, boy, but I need to know far more. I want you to go back and nick a van or something, and I want a report on the whole layout, in particular the secret cargo tunnel approaching it from cargo village to the passenger terminal.'

'I need time to research. I think there's a special permit for entering the cargo tunnel. And there's another little complication; I understand that the tunnel has television cameras along its whole length.'

'That's one of the things I want to know about. How they're placed and all that. A thorough job, Spider. No slip-ups. That's why I want *you*.'

All I could see was getting nicked. 'If there are cameras I'm going to be seen. I can't wear a stocking over my mug.'

'Then you work it out, boy. You're on a percentage of the take. One percent. And that will mean a handout of twenty thousand pounds. Now that can't be bad, can it, tax free?'

A two million pound snatch. Christ! what could it be?

Reisen looked across quizzically, suddenly a big man handling a big deal with the familiarity of experience. 'That's better than screwing a drum and peddling a bit of tom* round the fences, ain't it?'

'It wouldn't be much good to me on the Moor.'

'There you go again. Listen, boy, with the part you have to play, you won't even be breaking the law.'

'How long have I got?'

'This can't be rushed, Spider, boy. I know you've got to ask around first and I want the right answers. No chances. No ifs or buts. Wrong direction from you and we're all in it, which means that you finish up in a drum of quick-drying cement.'

'Supposing I say I've changed my mind.'

It took him by surprise. For a moment he stared then laughed quietly. 'You're a bit of a boy. You wouldn't have a mind left to change if I thought you meant that. No one opts out except feet first. You're in, Spider. Both the opera-

* Jewellery.

tions you have to do are by yourself. You're a loner – well, I've tried to keep it that way so you'll have no excuses afterwards.'

'Right. I'll do what I can.' What kind of idiot was I?

Now it was time to leave I was rooted. He had gone back to his mid-air focus act and I thought he was waiting for me to go when he said suddenly, 'They haven't got that bastard Chapman. He should have the acid dip – bit at a time.'

As I rose I was certain that he meant it. And I was bewildered. Floundering, I mumbled an agreement and got out.

Ray Lynch rang me at home that evening to say that he had come up with nothing bright on the Chapman background. Chapman's wife had gone to earth but judicious inquiry led to the belief that she was in a nursing home, suffering from shock, and receiving a quiet bit of treatment for her dipsomania. Anyway, she was out of circulation and nobody knew where she was, which indicated that she had something to tell.

For the next week I followed a routine. Every morning I went down to the airport. I wanted to get the feel of the place until I felt I belonged. By the end of that time I got to know the place better than my own office, mainly because I saw much more of it. I could have drawn a plan of the ticket counters, the offices, bookstalls, restaurants, bars, cafeterias and departure bays. I memorized every check point for getting airside to the aircraft. I located part of the cargo tunnel because there was a check point a little distance from a break in the tunnel. The guard, I noticed, invariably had his back to the tunnel due not only to the prevailing direction of the sparse traffic but also because of the position of his glass-topped box, as he was more concerned with vehicles going in than out. I quickly noticed that a road ran across the tunnel gap but I didn't dare get too close to the guard to see where it led.

The airport security vans were constantly on the move but with the bright diagonal runways on their side they were easily identifiable and therefore avoidable.

During this time I dug out every airline contact I had and delved into any extra information I could squeeze from them. Villains are good at painlessly extracting information; it's their stock in trade, a knack, like coppers interrogating.

As a familiarization course it was a success because I reached the point where I became addicted, I found myself missing the whine and roar of engines and the sight of planes lifting off or sinking low to straddle the deck.

Some evenings I made a point of seeing Penny. Most times we'd go out for a meal, which suited us both as we each lived alone. Penny was a gourmet and Fairfax had given me the seeds of learning when it came to food. Wines are different but with grub I was beginning to know my onions. We did a show but more often went back to her place to talk or make love and generally become much more emotionally involved with each other.

One evening I dropped in on Alan Bruce Chapman. I couldn't be sure that he would still be there and felt a bit of a fool giving the prearranged signal on the bedroom door. Yet he called out softly, 'Come in,' as if it were broad daylight and he was at home. I wondered if he realized the sensation he was causing beyond these walls; that he was the one man in the country that everyone knew about.

I went in silently from habit and the room was blacker than before. There was little cloud outside and there was a bit of a moon. Not liking it, I noticed that the window had disappeared. There was no light coming in at all. But over by the window wall I heard him scrabbling about. Then he called out, 'Switch your torch on, old chap.'

'What's going on?' I asked suspiciously, moving away from the point from where I'd spoken.

'What do you think's going on? I've blacked out the window.'

Cautiously I shone the torch downwards away from the window. True enough, hardboard covered the panes. He turned. 'I've had this up for the last four nights hoping you would come. It's worse than prison here, I get incredibly lonely. I prayed you'd come back.'

'Well, here I am.' I fished out a bag of boiled sweets and handed them over. In the diffused torchlight he had nothing of the proud looks of his photograph. And he was growing a beard. As I neared I could smell him and realized he could wash only infrequently because of the sound of running water; he still wore the same clothes.

Then I noticed that his shoes were off and he was only wearing one sock. He pointed to one end of the room; his shoes were propped up on their heels against the wall. Near them was his sock rolled into a ball. He smiled sheepishly. 'Been playing cricket,' he explained, 'mini wicket in the form of shoes and mini ball of socks stuffed with paper. Stops me going mad and gives me exercise.'

'Do you want me to bring you some socks?'

He stooped to retrieve the makeshift ball, unfolded it and put on the sock. 'Thanks but there's no need.'

Embarrassed by my stare he added, 'There's a completely new outfit sitting in the wardrobe but I've been told not to wear it yet. They told me to grow this beard too.' He fingered the untidy straggle that was emerging from stubble. It wasn't much of a beard and he had the wrong face for it.

We squatted while he unwrapped a sweet with trembling fingers.

'Why don't you put yourself out of your misery and just give yourself up?'

He was rolling the wrapper into a ball between finger and thumb and his cultivated tone rolled out around the sweet. 'I've often thought about it. But you know, once away from prison one is very reluctant to return to it.'

I knew how he felt. 'But this is far worse than nick.'

'I agree. But transitory. I can bear it for a little longer.' He started roaming the room.

'Have you found out any more? Who's behind it?'

'Not the Russians, I gather. That's an immense relief. Apparently an anonymous wellwisher is financing my escape. I don't pretend to understand but it seems that during the war I once did someone a favour important enough for him not to forget it.'

'Have you worked out who?'

'No. A lot happened during the war. What to me might have been trivia may have been particularly significant to someone else.'

It sounded tall to me and probably would have done to him had he not been reduced to such a pathetic state.

'Have you any idea when you're leaving here?'

He looked furtive, halting momentarily. 'No. Soon, I hope. I'm worried that the police may search empty houses.'

'They've already done this one. You're safe here. Where do you think they're sending you?'

He hesitated and started crunching his sweets, still holding the bag like a grubby little boy. 'I don't know,' he said finally.

'Come on. You know I could have turned you in long ago. Tell me, for God's sake.'

'I don't want you to know.'

I grinned. 'You go on like that and I'll take your sweets away.'

It was incredible. A week or two ago this man wouldn't have given me the time of day unless I had called him sir. Now he held the bag of sweets to his chest like a sulky kid. 'I can still shop you,' I threatened.

'India.'

'India?' I don't know why I was shaken. I simply hadn't been expecting it.

'How come?'

'I can work there. Apparently matters have been arranged.'

'What else has been arranged?'

'In a day or two I have to dress up for a photograph. They've told me to train my hair a different way.'

He caught me looking. 'Someone is coming to cut my hair for me; restyle it, I believe.'

All of this meant that they were rigging him up for a fake passport or they wouldn't need the photograph. It also indicated that they were taking him out openly. Brazenly? I'd learned a bit about the business since being in travel.

Change a man's appearance enough, book him an airline ticket in the ordinary way but under a false name, then arrange with the airline to VIP him, say as a director of some big company. Spin a yarn like it's the first time he's tried this particular airline and they'll hold his hand at the airport; take him to a special lounge while he's waiting; give him drinks, call him sir. *And they'd see that he boarded the aircraft before the other passengers.* It would work like a dream. Just who the hell would even begin to suspect that he was Alan Bruce Chapman?

'Do you hold an international certificate against smallpox?'

'There's one tucked in my passport but I hardly dare use that.'

'What about cholera? Have you been inoculated against it?'

'No. Why?'

'You need both those for travelling to India.' Seeing his face twitch and his eyes grow suspicious I added, 'Don't worry. The sort of people who are fixing this will know plenty of bent doctors.' Which was true but not the complete answer. It was queer.

I took a good long look at Alan Bruce Chapman. The torchlight was not being kind to his already sunken face. The light thrown from floor level dug deep shadows under his cheekbones and pushed his eyes back into wide hollows. Strains of light filtered through his beard, forming an untidy filigree. Once they had worked on him he would get away all right. Certain aspects of planning appeared sloppy but then I don't suppose he was intended to know too much. In spite of a couple of mild attempts at evasion I still reckoned that he was levelling with me. We had created an odd and unlikely relationship. A man in his position is glad of any sort of chat, anything momentarily to stave off fear and boredom. As he waited there day after day not really knowing what was happening his mind must turn inside out wondering how it would all end. I felt that he had been reduced to a cabbage not so much from fear but in the knowledge that his motive had been worthless; he had sacrificed himself for nothing.

'Why did your wife turn to drink?' I shot at him. It was cruel but effective.

He lost all colour and went rigid. 'What do you know about her?' His tone was coldly demanding; he was no longer thinking of himself.

'I heard she is being treated. Is that why you did it? To protect her when they got something on her? Did she step out of line so much that they could put the screws on you?'

He stood still in that unnatural posture created by the angle of his head which I later discovered was due to being thrown by a horse, and stared at me as if I was dirt. This was the man; dignified and hard and daring me to step out of line just once more. My God, his love for her must be strong.

His eyes clouded slightly and a little rigidity left his shoulders. 'I don't intend to discuss it.' Then he unbent a fraction. 'Alcoholism is a dreadful thing. Like drugs, it can make people act completely out of character.'

I reckoned I had scored a bull in one. The Ruskies must have exploited her condition until she was hopelessly involved. And he had done this for her. 'I'm sorry,' I said. 'I shouldn't have raised it. You must think the world of her.'

He didn't reply, and I wondered how he felt about it now.

When I left, mulling over the new information he had given me, I knew that he would welcome my return, his life having sunk to such small doubtful pleasures. Poor bastard.

CHAPTER 7

I saw young Charlie Hewitt at the office next morning before going down to the airport and asked him if he had had a booking to India recently. As Indian bookings didn't come up all that frequently he remembered instantly. 'Sure.

First class single.' He pulled out the file and produced the sales slip. 'Here we are. A Mr T. L. Ternat. It's a nibble from a possible new account. Big company, the Lomax Group. I've VIP'd him to try to swing it our way.'

I looked at the sales slip and saw that the reservation was to New Delhi in six days' time. I caught myself groaning and stiffened up when Charlie looked at me strangely.

'It's all right,' he said. 'It's been paid.'

'I can see that,' I said. 'Since when have business accounts settled in cash, particularly in a company of this size?'

Charlie looked hurt. 'They've never used us before. The booking came over the phone and they sent a messenger along with the money. I can't refuse payment, Mr Scott.'

'Of course you can't, but didn't you think it fishy that a big outfit should pay in this way? I mean, Christ, it's unusual, to put it mildly.'

'It's unusual all right, but who am I to argue? The booking is good, the money is good.'

'How's he getting back then? I mean, if he's supposed to be trying us out how the hell's he going to do that if he has no return?'

'He's unsure of his movements after Delhi. He has a UAT card.'

He would have, I thought. A Universal Air Travel card meant that he could buy a ticket against it anywhere in the world.

Charlie could see that I was still troubled and like the rest of us he didn't care for injustice. His young face was indignant as he said, 'I thought you'd be pleased. I can't understand the fuss about cash payment. Let's face it, Mr Scott, a lot of the business you've been bringing in lately has been settled in cash.'

That was nasty. Dead accurate but nasty. How could I explain to Charlie that most of our clients were villains and had opted out of the tax laws – at least partially.

'Give me a list of services to Delhi,' I demanded, sliding round his bull's eye. He passed me the air ABC. Not wanting to rouse Charlie's suspicions I did a job I should have got him to do. I looked up the flights to Delhi myself and in my ignorance missed a vital point.

'Did you remind him about vaccination and cholera?'

Charlie gave me a barely veiled look of contempt. 'I advised the girl who rang.'

I memorized the number of the Lomax Group and went into my own office. There I looked up the telephone directory to discover that their number was quite different from the one on the sales slip. There could be a lot of legitimate reasons for this but there was only one way of being sure. I rang up the Lomax number and asked for Mr Ternat. After some time I discovered that they had nobody of that name. I then rang the number of the sales slip and a skilled operator answered the phone by stating the number. I hung up. It was impossible for me to take it beyond this point without starting a scare.

So I tried another tack; after a bit of soft-soaping the inquiries operator I discovered that the number on the sales slip belonged to A. Lomax and Co Ltd. Clever. It could always be argued that Charlie Hewitt had understandably made a common mistake because I was willing to bet that there was no commercial connection between the two companies.

At the end of that week I moved in on the airside casing. So far I had received no pressure from Reisen but it seemed imminent. This time I took the overalls I had nicked rolled up under my arm. In the short tunnel leading to the aprons I slipped them on, then strode out.

The ceiling was low, thick grey cloud tumbling across the sky, swept by a long broom of wind that ruffled through my hair. A disembodied shriek of engines would be followed by a plane suddenly dropping from the murky shroud with tendrils of water vapour streaming under the flaps. Those taking off were quickly wrapped in the wet, clinging shroud.

I walked away from the mass of parked aircraft towards cargo village, heading for the perimeter boundary. There were fewer people over that side and the perimeter road led straight to the cargo tunnel.

All the time I sought forlornly for an abandoned car or van. Just behind me a tremendous roar of engines made me wish I had ear-pads, while away to my right that thick unhealthy sky swallowed and spewed planes every few seconds.

I stared across a desert of concrete on the far side of which was the last line of warehouses. Lines had been painted on the concrete for the guidance of aircraft and motor vehicles. It was a vast area of no-man's land, flat, exposed and uninviting. At the blind left-hand end of the long block a van was parked close to the wall; it seemed the most likely so I started walking across.

I must have appeared like a fly on a bare ceiling trying to be casual, feeling the strength of wind tearing at my clothes with no protection from the buildings, and wondering whether I was seen by people working at intervals along the row of sheds. I'd never felt so exposed in my life and I had the very strong feeling that I was breaking all the rules by going straight across. I just hoped that a sky giant didn't come trundling down towards me.

The strange thing about that concrete desert was my sudden need of water as my mouth went dry. Someone must have seen me approach and wondered what I was doing there.

The big doors of the end warehouse were drawn back both sides of the building so that I could see right through. At the rear was a loading platform and crates were being hoisted on to a truck. I strolled inside without causing a commotion and I suppose that there were about half a dozen shirt-sleeved Indians toiling away along the rows and rows of cargo shelves like some fantastic lost property office.

A smartly uniformed man stepped from between the shelves and gazed inquiringly at me. He had the complexion of Cuban mahogany and his heavy moustaches suggested ex-RAF or Indian Air Force. I recognized the insignia of Air India. He was gazing at me pleasantly enough but waiting for me to explain myself.

'It looks like I've got the wrong place,' I said genially. 'I'm looking for Harry McNally of Air Canada.'

'Air Canada? Then you've come too far.' He pointed a gold-banded arm towards the bulk of cargo sheds and explained the way to me.

'You haven't got a van going that way?' I asked hopefully.

He grinned; white teeth under the jet black moustaches. 'There will be but in about an hour. The driver's just gone over to the Rising Sun for lunch. You'll have to walk.'

I thanked him and went round the end of the shed as if towards the perimeter road. There was the van, the sliding door variety. On its windscreen was what I had learned to be the most precious pass of all; a yellow disc with the letters CT boldly black at its centre. CT : Cargo Tunnel. For the tunnel it was not the personnel who required a permit but the vehicles.

The perimeter road in front of me curved slowly round the rear of the main sheds. In the middle of the road two parallel yellow lines marked the airport boundary as if carrying some precious power to stop people crossing them. On the other side of the road, just a few yards from me and outside the airport precincts, was a small private car park. Very handy.

I slid back the nearside door of the van, climbed in, released the catch, then opened the bonnet and applied one of the few things I always carry while on a job, a crocodile clip. I got back in and started her, releasing the clip and closing the bonnet with careful pressure. In the driver's seat I was afraid that those inside the shed would hear the running engine. Yet I had to sweat it out; better to be caught now than in or near the tunnel. So I let the engine idle for a minute or two and waited.

Pushing her into low gear I pulled slowly away from that wall and cut diagonally on to the road. There was no sign of activity in my mirror so I kept her rolling nice and slow even when one of the Airport Authority cars raced past.

I was jittery as I neared the tunnel entrance, where a

89

guard was coming to life. I was committed. Ahead of me stretched the tunnel and another spell in nick if I didn't make it.

From habit the guard glanced up at the windscreen and noted the all-important pass. I was pressed well back in the seat wearing the overalls, which were proving to be a godsend.

Suddenly I was in. Ostensibly it was just another underground pass. The lighting wasn't particularly good, but through this tunnel passed a variety of valuable cargoes in vans like this fetching and carrying to and from the warehouses and aircraft. If a cargo was particularly valuable then a security car would follow the van. And to insure against a snatch a series of cylindrical television cameras were fixed high up, facing both ways so that all vehicles were watched and recorded.

It was a nasty feeling knowing that every inch of my progress was being seen and the van number was noted. So I kept at snail pace, keeping my head well back and trying to remember the positions of cameras. Any attempt at a snatch in here must fail.

Ahead of me the tunnel began to bear left. So soon? Then I saw open road and realized I'd reached the break in the tunnel that I'd spotted from outside. There was too much to see at once and my eyes were revolving on stalks as I tried to take it all in. I saw the guard's checkpoint with the double open gates obliquely to my right. His back was towards me, as his job was to check incoming traffic. As I entered the gap daylight flooded over me and to my immediate right I saw a road that could take me straight out of the airport perimeter. But what spurred me most as I tried to recall this was that I was certain I had located a blind spot in the TV network on the curve of the tunnel. I couldn't be sure. I dared not stop.

Before I could sort myself out I was in the second half of the tunnel which was curving all the way like a quarter-circle. There were no weaknesses in the television set-up here and I couldn't be certain that I had been right about the other sector. There was only one way to be sure and that was to go back.

I emerged into the open to the right of the main warehouse block. The cloud was still low, molten lead dripping its waste. I couldn't go straight back in and I couldn't hang around either, so I did a little tour, getting in nobody's way, gave it a few minutes then pushed off.

Back into the tunnel I wondered if those TV scanners thought it odd that I was returning so soon. This time I was keyed up as I approached the gap. It was a vital point. And as I entered the tunnel again I knew for sure that I was right about the blind spot. Just on the bend and in my mirror I could see that the guard was also out of sight at this particular point. They must know the blind spot existed.

Once outside I could see the Air India shed. Veering left I approached the warehouse on its blind end, scanning the ground between the road and the Rising Sun in case matey suddenly popped up and caught me. I parked her where she had been before. I climbed out and walked back down the road a bit; then I crossed it and let myself out of the airport perimeter.

Reisen gave me his full attention but I wasn't satisfied. Something was wrong.

The plan I had drawn was spread over his desk as I described the layout to him. While he listened attentively to everything I had to say I somehow got the impression that his probing questions were emphasizing the wrong points. Still, it was his party. Even so, something of his undoubted organizing ability rubbed off as he went over the plan time and again until I felt certain that he knew it better than I did. He was pleased, too; he didn't say so then but his eyes were bright with interest. He knew what I was saying and winkled out the doubtful points. His thoroughness produced my first spark of respect for him. Slipping his cigar back into his mouth he drew on it until his cheeks hollowed. Rolling up the plan he tapped me on the shoulder with it.

'You've done a good job, Spider. That's what I call casing.' He knew I was waiting for more so he strolled round his office as if he was redesigning it, stooped to look at the military medal and his photographs, perhaps by now recognizing himself in one of them, then turned dramatically and pointed his cigar at me.

'It'll be just a few days now. Don't go away for the next week or two. Knocker will be in touch to give you a briefing. OK?'

I nodded. 'Isn't it time you opened up a bit?' I queried.

He stared hard. His own boys didn't speak to him like this. Then he grinned. 'Once a loner, always a loner, eh, Spider, boy?' He sauntered back to his desk and eyed me speculatively. 'How do you think I stay out of trouble? Leave the planning to me, boy. You'll know in time and it won't be long.'

And this puzzled me. Reisen was a very careful, very effective planner from all I heard. He didn't rush things. His boys were well rehearsed. You can't be well rehearsed at short notice.

I met Penny that night. There was a lot of tension I wanted to get rid of and it was just possible that she might have a bit more to say about Reisen.

The placards were still filled with Chapman and I felt sorry for him because that's how it had been with me. It was still the hottest news. In Penny's cottage she slipped off her shoes and we were back to normal.

Her gaze fell on a folded *Evening News*. Like the posters the banner was about Chapman. 'What do you think of someone like him?' Somehow it irritated me.

'How should I know? I've never met him.'

'Yes, but the sort of thing he's done. Don't be bloody awkward, Willie.'

'I'm not. I don't like people being prejudged.'

'Let me put it another way,' she went on. 'Supposing he's guilty. Supposing he's given stuff to the Ruskies. Now you, with your reputation of being the great non-grasser of all time, if you could put your finger on him would you shop him?'

It was much too near the mark. She was ferreting.

I gazed at her but there was nothing but innocent inquiry in her face and that impish challenge in her eyes.

'I think I'd shop him,' I said. 'He knows far too much for all our sakes. I think I'd have to.'

She came over to me then, sensuous and teasing. As she wriggled close to me she rubbed noses and said, 'So would I, my darling. So would I.'

I didn't get back until the early hours. Shortage of sleep didn't stop the Special Branch boys from rousing me at seven thirty.

It's an old police trick to call early while your brain is still addled; you give something away before you realize it. But old lags are used to this. There was a hammering on my door and I poddled over in bare feet and crumpled pyjamas. There they stood. Tweedledum and Tweedledee, Detective Chief Superintendent Newbound raising his hat slightly, an amusing glint in his eye. Sergeant Chittle looked his usual baleful self.

'For God's sake,' I exploded. 'It's the middle of the night.' And began to close the door. Chittle put his big foot in the gap so I gave it a nasty squeeze.

'Just a word, Mr Scott, sir.' Newbound said it beautifully, this boy had seen the lot. I liked his style. So I let him in.

Chittle grabbed my chair before I could stop him and I felt like a foreigner in my own room. I was still befuddled through lack of sleep or I would have had him out of it. Standing there dishevelled, undressed and unshaven, they virtually had the drop on me.

'We still want to know why you phoned that number, Spider.'

'Get stuffed,' I said with the authority of practice. It all came down to basics in the end.

'Any man,' replied Newbound levelly, 'who's done the amount of bird you have must be pretty thick. Now don't make yourself a bigger chump than you already are.' Chittle just sat leering his opinion of me.

I almost told them; almost broke my own golden rule about grassing to coppers. It wasn't ethics that stopped me but the simple safety of my own skin. I trusted Newbound. I didn't trust Chittle. I could be wrong on both counts. Either way it didn't really matter. All I knew was that Reisen had bent coppers on his payroll.

And *that* I couldn't answer.

'You're forgetting we're Special Branch, Spider,' said Newbound quietly. 'I know we're coppers but we're not after crime. You know what we want.'

'It's no use.'

Newbound glared angrily. 'You can't expect Fairfax to come trotting out every time some old lag of a creeper thinks he has something to say. Let us check it out for him.'

I turned to him and shook my head sadly. 'You nearly had me going,' I said. 'It was a good shot that hurt. Better luck next time.'

He nodded; a good loser. 'Come on, Sergeant,' he said, and put on his hat. Chittle rose, not understanding what was going on. They left quietly.

At the office I found the three counter staff fully busy and in my own office another small desk had been squeezed in beside Lulu's and a blonde-haired girl of about seventeen was hard at a new typewriter. Her age was all that was young about her; by the time I had penetrated the myriad of pencil lines round her eyes, the heavy silver on her lids and the purple brushed around the whole eye area I was able to see that she had a promiscuous gaze that viewed me like the entry of Methuselah after a night on the tiles. She went on chewing gum and didn't look at me again, which was as well as I felt inclined to hang her on the wall as a piece of surrealistic painting. Her name was Marge. I never discovered her other name.

Knocker Roberts rang me that afternoon; would I meet him at the foot of Nelson's Column at five?

It was a good place to meet if dry, and it was. The pigeons were swooping about like fighter planes. The square was loosely crowded and Nelson rode high in the sunlight, a constant target for unerringly accurate aerial bombardment from his feathered friends, which was as well with so many people about.

Knocker pitched up with the low sun shadowing the craters on his face and making him squint on his hacked up side.

'Nice day, Knock.'

'Yeah! About bloody time. Let's go up to the parapet where we can talk.' He led the way up the wide stone steps beyond the fountains where some wag had dropped purple dye into the water. We walked along to a central position, then leaned on the stone balustrade to face Trafalgar Square below us like some huge stage with us viewing it from the backcloth prop of a balcony. With the fountains playing and leaves sprouting fresh green from the plane trees it should have been pleasant.

Knocker said, 'The job's on, whack.'

I couldn't see any other reason why he had come so I kept quiet. I noticed I had landed his bad side again and that the sun was anointing him with another halo.

'It's on the twentieth,' added Knocker to the pigeons. 'The exact time has still to be checked but you'll be told. OK?'

I nodded, thinking that the ticket to Delhi for Mr T. L. Ternat was for the 17th.

'What's the snatch?' I asked, watching a pigeon alight on a girl's head and send her screaming.

'Better that you don't know, mate. You're not on that side of it.'

'Don't give me that, Knocker. If I'm risking nick then I'm on every side of it.'

'Your job's easy. You've already done the hard bit. You'll be on the getaway van.'

'Getaway van? I'm a craftsman not a racing driver.'

He turned with what was meant to be a reassuring look of appreciation. 'And so you are, old matey. You're a bloody good driver too.'

95

'Christ! After all the build-up this is what I land.'

'Don't underestimate it, Spider. You'll have to drive as you've never driven before, but the stake is high.'

'It had better be. I'm on a percentage.'

'Is that a fact? Rex only does that with the top people. Can you remember the plan you drew up for him?'

'I'm unlikely to forget it.'

'Opposite the Air India cargo shed, just outside the perimeter, is that small car park. All you have to do is to park a van there and stay with it until the boys pitch up with the cargo. Keep the rear doors of the van unlatched so they can throw it in, climb in themselves and then away.'

'How many of them will there be?'

'Two.'

I faced him in surprise. 'Two? What sort of snatch is it?'

'It doesn't have to be heavy to be valuable. Some of the boys will have dropped off. Once the job is done we only need two leg men to get it over to you.'

Reisen had been talking of a two million pound snatch. Somehow it didn't sound right.

'Anything else?' I asked, as uneasy as I'd ever been.

'No, whack. I'll ring and give you the registration number, colour and location of the van and the time to be there. You haven't even got to nick one.'

'What about where I'm supposed to drive to after the snatch?'

He grinned. 'You don't need to remember that. One of the lads will direct you when they reach the van.'

'And if they don't?'

'Then you've nowhere to go, matey.'

After I had left him I walked the few yards back to the shop. By now it was closed so I unlocked the Chubb lock with my little golden key – you can't trust anyone these days – and went behind the counter. Charlie Hewitt was a meticulous worker. I opened the drawer where he kept his booking files in date order of departure and rifled through them. There it was, T. L. Ternat, departing 17th May. I opened the file, examined it and put it back. All roads had been leading to Rome and now suddenly they were bypassing it. I was foxed.

CHAPTER 8

I dropped in on Alan Bruce Chapman about half past midnight. This time I'd taken one of those little electric candle lights so that I could put it on the ground between us. He was edgy, plucking at his skin like a junkie, but he seemed glad to see me. His beard had grown a bit and his hair now looked quite different. With the amount of weight he'd lost through worry and privation I guessed that he'd pass for someone else without much trouble.

I gave him his sweets. He seemed to accept them reluctantly. He'd given up playing cricket; his shoes were on.

'Any more news?' I asked him, when we were settled down Indian-fashion.

'About what, old boy?'

I had wondered when the politician would begin to show.

'You know what. When are you moving out?'

'I don't know yet.'

'Well, have they taken your photograph yet?'

He decided that this was all right and told me that they had but that he had not yet seen the passport.

'Have you ever heard of someone called T. L. Ternat?' I slipped in as he unwrapped another sweet.

His hands stopped moving for a couple of seconds and it was surprising how much noise the unravelling paper had been making in the empty room. As his fingers moved again the cellophane crackled like static.

'It's not a name I remember. Has it some significance?'

What had made him so suddenly assured? He was only a flicker of the political flame he had been only days ago but was more in command of himself as if he knew what was going to happen and was unafraid of it.

'You've got to use a pseudonym to get out of the country. I wondered if that was it.'

'If it is I have not been informed.'

They wouldn't give him a name at the last moment – he needed to get used to it.

'Aren't you curious that I'm asking you?'

'Very curious. But I have to bear in mind that ours is an odd association. Even now I don't know why you're here. You see, you hold my life in your hands; I don't want to offend you in any way.'

He was bang in form. With the return of assurance his sincerity had gone. He was used to slipping awkward questions in the House of Commons but they were now being asked by an amateur so he found it all so easy. What had happened to the scared rabbit? I went over to the wardrobe to examine his suit. As it was dark that side of the room I had to go back for the lamp.

'What are you doing?' he demanded acidly.

'I'm wondering why you've stopped levelling with me. So I thought I'd see for myself. I can still shop you, you know.'

'Don't you think I know that? I'm being perfectly honest with you.' A little of his earlier fear crept back.

He made no attempt to stop me searching the suit. There was nothing in the pockets but I couldn't believe that he didn't know his new identity.

'Haven't you asked them what name you'll be travelling under?'

The suit was in the fifty-sixty guinea range – a director's suit all right.

'Of course. I'm curious to know. But they seem to think the less I know at this stage the safer all round.'

It was plausible but not good enough. They couldn't risk the chance of a slip-up at the airport. 'And you're still going to India?'

'I've heard nothing to the contrary.' He was wary of me

again as he was at our first meeting. But then he had been scared silly; now he was cautious, as if he had been warned. I knew I couldn't beat him at the evasion game. Before I went back to him I noticed that the tailor's label had been removed from the suit.

'This is my last visit,' I explained to him. 'I'll keep out of your hair.' I picked up the lamp and the shadows deepened under his eyes.

'I shall miss you, Mr Burglar. I've enjoyed your visits; they've helped me retain my sanity.'

I believe he meant it. But I also believed that it was the first touch of honesty I had heard from him that evening. Looking down at him I noticed that he had his eyes averted as if to avoid the glare of the light.

'Have you told anyone about me?'

He looked up startled. 'Good Lord, no. We agreed. Anyway, I dare not risk it. I don't know what their reaction would be; perhaps disastrous for me.'

I wasn't convinced. 'And of course a gentleman always keeps his word.'

'Naturally.'

In his eyes why should I be afraid? I hadn't sprung him.

Neither of us made a move to shake hands when I left; neither had the inclination. I knew my reason but wondered about his. The man had changed during our brief acquaintance. When I finally left it was with a very uncomfortable feeling. I simply couldn't see where it was all leading except perhaps to one big packet of trouble for me. Why the hell did I have to have an extra Y chromosome? Why couldn't I be like everyone else and enjoy watching television?

I went back to my bedsitter to salvage what remained of the night. I could opt out if I happened to be that kind of animal but I knew for a certainty that I'd been netted neatly for some reason so obscure that I was nowhere near it. It wasn't my fault that Fairfax avoided me; he knew the type of person I was, knew my loyalties and my distrusts. If Chapman escaped, Fairfax could take the consequences. I'd done what I could within my own codes.

The next morning I was slipping out of the office for a quiet lunch when young Charlie Hewitt called me.

'Mr Scott.' And as I returned to the counter, 'You still interested in that Ternat booking?'

'Mildly, Charlie. What's on?'

'He's changed his date. They nearly all do but I thought you had a personal interest in this one.' Good for Charlie.

'What's the change?'

'Put it back a few days. He's now travelling on the twentieth.'

The twentieth! That hammered me straight between the eyes.

'You sure?' It was all I could get out.

He gave that experienced look of his that condemned all lay employers as half-baked idiots. 'Of course I'm sure.'

'Where does the plane finally go? I mean after Delhi?'

'Bombay. That's the end of its run under that flight number.'

It didn't help much. 'Doesn't go anywhere else?' I was really groping for something I didn't recognize.

'Moscow, en route.'

'What?' I coughed quickly. 'Moscow? That's a funny route for Delhi.'

'No, it's quicker actually. Few airlines are allowed that way. London, Moscow, straight down over the Samarkand desert, over Afghanistan and the Western Himalayas, then Delhi. It's a very good service.'

'I thought the Russians were fussy about who flies over their country.'

Charlie grinned. 'They are. The Russian bit is all done at night.'

Bloody Moscow. It had been under my nose. 'It wasn't shown in the Air ABC,' I said weakly.

'Yes it was, Mr Scott. You probably looked up London/ Delhi. Complete routings in the three letter code are in another section.' He could afford to smile blithely at his chump of a boss.

'Thanks, Charlie.' And then I had an idea. 'Won't some-one have to bring the ticket back to be changed?'

But it was Charlie's day. 'No. They're having it revalidated at the airport.'

I didn't go far outside. Once out of sight of the shop I leaned against the nearest wall and felt the stirring of fear. There was going to be no snatch at London Airport. It was going to be a dummy, that's why it sounded so soft. They wanted a diversion to get Chapman away. And it tied Reisen in tightly. But would he do something that would be abhorrent to him even for money? And why drag me in?

I was jittery. It was all about to break and I had the nasty feeling that it would crash about me. Get the concentration of security at London Airport fluttering round the wrong spot for the bird to flee from another. It was sound. Some-one would have to leak the false snatch so that the police and Airport Authority were alerted. Which could endanger some of the boys if they were running a dummy. Perhaps there weren't going to be any boys. Except one. Muggins waiting in the car park just outside the perimeter in what was almost certainly a stolen van. By the time that the security forces had sorted it out and had come up with me as a lone prisoner Alan Bruce Chapman would be en route for Moscow.

Poor old Chapman was going to have his head squeezed dry by the Russians after all. The poor mug had been sold down the river. He would have been better off in an English nick; at least he'd get three regular meals a day and a bed without flashing lights and interminable interviews until his mind was turned inside out. I had to warn him. And it couldn't wait until night.

The 'For sale' sign was still outside so I went through the gate as if I had come to view. Round the back I realized that I couldn't enter by my usual window because as soon as I climbed on to the shed I would be visible from the side street. I waited until I could hear no footsteps then sharply hit one of the panes in the kitchen door with my elbow. The falling glass made a racket so I waited again, then plucked out one or two jagged slivers before putting my hand through to turn the key. The door opened and I stepped over the mess of glass on the kitchen floor.

I went up the stairs two at a time. I gave the usual signalled tap before entering in case I frightened the life out of him. The room was empty. I had acted dangerously coming here, risking bumping into the people who briefed and fed Chapman and my reward was bare walls.

I couldn't believe it. Standing in the open doorway I gazed around and it was as though none of it had ever happened. The camp bed had gone. There was no board to cover the window at night. The wardrobe was closed. There was not only no sign of life but absolutely no indication that anyone had been here as recently as last night. For a moment I thought I was going round the twist. I went over to the wardrobe and pulled back its doors. The suit had gone – if there had ever been one; Chapman's presence had been so eliminated that I was left wondering about myself.

Then I got a bit of sense back and walked slowly round the room looking for traces. He must have gone just after I left. No wonder he had been cagey. But the absence of the camp bed indicated that he'd had help. It had all been arranged before I pitched up. So he had lied. Had he grassed on me? The strong possibility made my blood run cold.

I went out on to the landing and lowered the ladder to the loft. Certain that there was no one up there I climbed the ladder and pushed up the trap door. My pencil torch uncovered one clue that it had not been all a dream. The blackout board had been returned to where it came from. But that was all.

So Chapman was going to finish up in Moscow. There was nothing else I could do about it. Fairfax had let me down. And I was utterly confused by Reisen's involvement.

The only alternative was that all I had heard and learned about Reisen was bunk. He'd been kidding everybody. I searched the house as if I was looking for a needle just to get some clue of where Chapman might have gone. It didn't surprise me that I came up with nothing but I vented my spleen on the search. One cosy little item I discovered; the whisky glass that Reisen had threatened me with was resting among some empty tins in the kitchen cabinet. Nice bastard. I wondered how long it had been there. I cleaned it and put it back, so that was one threat removed. But it didn't explain why he had put it there. My skin was on shifting cinders by the time I left that place.

Back at the office I lugged out an Air India timetable and studied it as if I knew what I was at. The 20th was a Thursday. On that date Flight AI506 left London at 1700 hours for Moscow, Delhi and Bombay. In the opposite column I idly noticed that Flight AI507 coming from Bombay and Delhi arrived London just about one and a half hours before the other one took off. It was not a turnaround; not the same plane. It would now be interesting to see what time Knocker wanted me at the airport.

Lulu brought me a late cup of coffee with a look that suggested I'd been overdoing things. Marge put me beyond the pale and offered me nothing but a keep-at-arm's-length-dad glance that made me feel my age. While I sipped at the hot mud-like drink I was visualizing old Chapman sitting in the plane prior to take-off; hearing the stewardess announce the stopover at Moscow. But there would be someone with him to see that he didn't leave his seat. And then into the transit lounge at Sheremetyevo Airport to drink warm, indifferent beer and watch the rest of the passengers waiting, like himself, for the onward journey. Only there wouldn't be one for him. He would be whisked out of that little patch of no-man's-land into Soviet Russia and the Western World wouldn't hear from him again. From time to time the British press would print rumours from reliable sources. Officialdom would be worried sick and try to play down the whole affair while they desperately speculated on what Chapman had coughed up. They would have to take the worst view and accept that some irreparable damage had been done and would try to anticipate Soviet attitudes. By this time Chapman would be a shell, a cabbage or a corpse.

With a feeling of utter dejection I again rang Fairfax's

old number but it was hopeless. Now more than ever I was unwilling to talk to the fuzz; I was walking a knife's edge. I wasn't too good at hiding my depression from the staff, but then I've never been that hot at hiding my feelings.

I was meeting Penny that evening and almost put it off. Then I saw it as a last opportunity of doing a little prying before I was stuffed on the altar of a tiny car park.

I asked her if she was still planning on leaving Reisen.

'I'm a determined lass. Why?'

I got her off my knees and she pulled at her skirt hem as she realized I was serious. 'What would you say if I said I was doing a job for Reisen?'

'I'm not in a position to criticize; but I'd be disappointed.'

Letting it ride I asked, 'Have you heard any more about this snatch at Heathrow?'

'I know the date.'

'Tell me.'

'I don't think I should.'

'Tell me,' I snapped. 'I'm in on it.'

'Oh, no! The twentieth.'

'Tell me this. Reisen's image has always been that he's the great patriot. Bent as a scorpion's tail but with a strange loyalty to the Crown, like me in fact. Do you believe it's true?'

'He's not likely to discuss it with *me*. I don't know. It could be true.'

'Does he know that we're seeing each other?'

'He's bound to. It's none of his business.'

It could be, I thought. He wasn't beyond imparting his tit-bits in front of Penny in the hope of them reaching me. I didn't suggest this to her; she still worked for him and loyalties had peculiar outlets, as I well knew.

'I'm sorry to hear you're in on the job,' she said quietly. 'I thought you had broken clean; inspired me to do the same, dear Willie.'

'Perhaps there will be no job,' I said hopefully.

'Oh, there'll be one all right. And if you're in there's no way out. What on earth made you do it?'

I couldn't tell her about Chapman. It was all too involved and she wouldn't understand my double game against Reisen. And if I was doubling him, just what was he doing with me? 'Money,' I said.

She shrugged eloquently. 'That's the usual reason,' she agreed without recrimination. That was one thing about her; she met so many villains that she knew what it was all about; there were no feminine tantrums. But I couldn't help wondering why she was so emphatic that the snatch was on at a time I had convinced myself that it didn't exist at all.

She lifted her hand to me and I held her fingers. She smiled a little wistfully and said, 'I'm very fond of you, Willie; I shall be sorry if anything happens to you.'

Knocker phoned me next morning and we met like a couple of clandestine lovers under the shadow of Nelson who had seen it all with his one eye. This time I grabbed a carton of seed for the pigeons and fed them while he spoke.

Watching me throwing the seed he observed, 'You're soft on animals, ain'tcher, whack?'

'I'm soft, period.' The birds were beginning to perch on my head and arms.

'Hope you can afford a new suit, mate.' Then he said, 'You must be in that car park by three at the very latest. The very latest,' he stressed again. He handed me over car keys on a hook with a plastic tab. 'The van's number is ISS 1467C. It's grey. It's a Ford. And it will be parked on a parking meter in Northumberland Avenue on the twentieth. All you have to do is to get in and drive it.'

'Say the number again.'

He did and he left me to the pigeons who came winging in on their own private airport.

The next few days were bewildering. I wished there was someone I could trust enough to chew things over with. In the end it all came back to the fact that once a loner always a loner. But it didn't stop me dreading the twentieth. I tried the King Canute stunt and ordered it not to but it pitched up in a fine drizzle on a grey May morning just the same.

The London sparrows' version of a dawn chorus was tweeting away when I rose, with a blackbird doing the solos. The feeling I had was that if I made a balls-up, and that could be achieved simply by going, then I would either be tucked away for a good number of years or would belatedly make a race of it down the Thames with Ossie Jenkins.

The weather didn't help. The muck splashed up over the car and sprayed the windscreen with soft mud pellets as I drove down the short stretch of the Bayswater Road towards Oxford Street. There wasn't much on the road yet. In an hour the streets would be crammed. I parked in Selfridge's garage, walked hatless to the Tube at Oxford Circus and caught the Bakerloo Line down to Trafalgar Square. By this time my clothes were soggy, my trousers clinging round my knees. It didn't improve my mood. At Trafalgar Square I crossed the Strand at the traffic lights. And I walked slowly down Northumberland Avenue, keeping close to the buildings for as much protection as I could get from the heavy rain.

I was lucky. The grey van was on this side of the street parked outside the Standard Bank of South Africa. Inappropriately leaning against the wall of the bank with raincoat collar turned up and a wet floppy hat over the coal-black face was a West Indian I knew who tried to avoid my glance.

'Hello, Smoky,' I greeted him warmly, huddling against the wall with him. 'Trying for a takeover?'

He grinned crookedly, a small elephant's tusk below the dripping beam of his hat. 'Hell, no, man, I ain't got that sort o' money.' His humorous dark eyes flashed backwards in a glance towards the bank. 'I wouldn't leave my money there in case they split it down the middle.' But it was said without rancour. Smoky Joe West held rancour for no man and almost everyone took advantage of it.

I nodded towards the grey van just in front of us. 'How much time left on the meter?'

He gave me the wide-eyed innocent stare and no man did it better. 'What you on about, man?'

'Come off it, Smoky. One of Reisen's boys told you to deliver the van and hang around to make sure I picked it up.'

'No, man. No, sir, Spider. I'm just out for a walk.'

Looking at his dripping clothes I laughed. 'How long you been with Reisen?'

'Nothing permanent, jus' casual labour.'

'Keep away from him. You don't want to hurt your wife and kids.'

'I've no work right now, man. I gotta do somethin'.'

'Yeah, well, if I come through the day give me a ring tomorrow.' I gave him a card. 'It'll only be as general runaround but it'll keep you out of trouble until you find something better. OK?'

'You offerin' me a job, Spider, man?'

'Sort of a job. Better than this one you're doing.'

'Thanks, man.'

'What's on the clock? I don't want to get wetter than I am already.'

'There's over half an hour left, man.'

The poor blighter had been hanging around for about an hour and a half. He had a sort of natural dignity and basic pride that forbade him to stand in the bank's doorway.

'Come on,' I said. 'I'll buy you a cup of coffee. Then you can report back to Knocker Roberts that you delivered and I collected.' We turned into Deno's next door to Lawson's the hairdresser.

Twenty minutes later I approached the van on my own. The rain had eased a little but I was already wet enough not to care. There it was in a moderate state of cleanliness, ISS 1467C. The registration plate looked about the same age as the van; it had been well done. As I looked it over I was full of the unshakeable feeling that this van and I were about to start a meaningful association. I felt that I had an attachment to it like a patient with a doctor; we would mean something to each other before the day was out.

The meter was almost at zero. I scanned the area for lurking traffic wardens before feeding the meter with a bunch of tanners. Then I walked away.

CHAPTER 9

I was glad when it was time to move. By midday I was dried out with an early lunch inside me and felt a little more human. The streets were still wet but the rain had stopped and the cloud ceiling was beginning to lift and scatter. I drove along crowded Piccadilly towards fashionable Knightsbridge. I was worried, morose and cautious without knowing what the hell I was supposed to look out for. I was driving into trouble but if I didn't go I'd still be up to my neck in it; Reisen didn't gladly suffer let-downs.

I approached the airport with the care of doing a breaking-and-entering job and felt slightly sick in the pit of my stomach.

As I was early I circled the airport twice, hearing aircraft whining in the cloud as if lost. Then finally I came up the perimeter road, left of the double yellow lines, looking for the small car park opposite the Air India shed in cargo village. I had a moment of fright when it suddenly occurred to me that there might not be parking space. But there were two or three empty bays and I trundled into the one best placed for a getaway. I was fifteen minutes early.

For some time I followed orders and stayed where I was. But I was so uneasy that eventually I climbed out to take stock. Everything looked the same this side of the double yellow lines as it did the other. It was now three-thirty and I had no idea how long I was supposed to wait.

My inclination was to get as far away from this car park as I could. I wanted to see if Chapman got away but the flight didn't take off until five. As time passed I became more uneasy because I was conspicuous by the van; I knew I had been noticed by some of the cargo village personnel across the road. Staying in the driver's seat was like staying in solitary but that was what I should have done.

After half an hour I reckoned I had stayed long enough. If the job was so badly timed that I had to hang around for so long then I was either right about there being no job or it had come to grief. Yet I had heard no police sirens and when I considered it had seen little sign of London Airport Authority vehicles.

At half-past four my urge to leave was overwhelming. I had waited almost two fruitless hours and reckoned by now that I could reasonably leave my post without recrimination. Slipping the ignition key into my pocket I crossed the yellow lines and headed for the main block of warehouses across the concrete desert. This time I wasn't wearing my overalls but nobody stopped me. My old Army training made me feel like a sentry deserting his post, but my creeper's training whispered to me that I was playing it right, avoiding a trap, no matter how obscure. I don't walk out on jobs; I simply didn't believe that there was any kind of job except getting Chapman away and I wasn't necessary for that.

I was further concerned when I saw no signs of distress around the Pan Am sheds and they were the boys who were supposed to be on the wrong end of the snatch. So that was that. Reisen had in some way set me up but it had gone wrong.

I suppose I should have turned back then and driven away. I didn't. I kept going towards the departure lounge at the third terminal as if I was being wound in by someone there. What made it more fascinating was the Air India Boeing 707 alongside for embarkation of passengers.

Standing there against the north wall of number three building I slunk back as far as I could. There was a lot of activity, other aircraft like foil-wrapped gifts scattered about, but the scene was different from my last visit. There seemed to be more aircraft, more vehicles, more mechanics and officials. Then I noticed loose concentrations of Airport

Authority vehicles idling around in all sorts of places. A large number of mechanics were just pottering, seemingly making work. No wonder air fares are high.

And then I had it. The place was lousy with coppers. Had I been nearer I would have known sooner. The extra vans, coppers dressed as mechanics all round the departure area but nothing really happening. If any one of them had a nose like mine he would soon spot my presence and ask what the hell I was doing there. Yet I couldn't move. Chapman couldn't have been taken off because the whole atmosphere was one of waiting.

They must have been tipped off or they wouldn't be there. Passengers were still filing out; the little starter truck was under the nose of the Boeing and the engineer was walking round the under-belly of the plane making his pre-flight inspection. It all looked so normal; yet it was not.

At this time all thought of Reisen and his van had left me. I couldn't understand what was happening. This couldn't be for Chapman, I thought; they would have had him by now. And yet at any moment I expected the great concentration of security to ring the plane. When the last passenger was on board and the doors were closed and locked, still nothing happened and I thought I was going bonkers. For God's sake stop him going, I called out wordlessly. No one heard me. The crazy scene went its crazy way and coppers searched for work to look part of this unreal tableau.

When the port engines of the Boeing fired the plane itself was studiously ignored. I had to be wrong. This simply did not make sense. But it was happening. The Boeing was slowly taxiing away, her engines almost idling in a shrill whine as she slowly swung round towards the taxiing lanes. There were other planes shrieking away but I had ears only for the one with the Air India insignia striped down her flanks and up her tail and nosing her way behind a BOAC VC10 to queue up for take-off.

And still there was no action from this very substantial concentration of security forces. I thought, well, that's that, and something went out of me but I couldn't take my eyes off the machine. Then she swung slowly round again so that she was facing me port side on and I could see her magnificent lines. My gaze fastened to her as if I was hypnotized. Fairfax had really bodged this one, I thought desperately. Then she stopped almost opposite me, the engines subdued to a healthy whistle that suddenly cut out in a subsiding slide down the scale.

It was like a signal. The engines died and the stationary vehicles came to life in a bizarre game of musical chairs as they interwove to form a rough circle around the plane. The overalled coppers suddenly took interest and spread out, some in my direction. It was too late to run. Had I really wanted to I don't think my legs would have moved; there was something immensely compelling about the whole scene. The props were being moved and something new was emerging.

Two overalled coppers went past me with hardly a glance, assuming that I had a right to be there. I sidled a little nearer to the alleyway that led to the Air India office within the building in case I had to do a bunk. Some mechanics had manoeuvred to the starboard side of the plane and it was ringed as effectively as a dove.

It now seemed clear that the whole plan had been to isolate the plane so that passengers were settled and Chapman couldn't try a dash back through the crowded departure lounge. It was going to be all nice and discreet. Poor bastard.

The embarkation steps were being trundled into position at the first-class entrance. The plane waited like a well-trained setter, as the sun explored a crack in the cloud and flashed down the silver body like a bolt of lightning. The steps were fastened and two plainclothes men stepped forward and slowly mounted them. The cabin door was pulled back as they reached the platform and I could see a serious-faced stewardess hovering in the aperture. Stepping inside, the coppers disappeared while the door remained open. At the bottom of the steps two copper-mechanics stood guard.

The sun was still casting incandescence along the top of the fuselage as though it was on fire. Then the cloud plunged out the light and the plane looked sullen. Shadows appeared behind the open door but only as a slow confusion of movement. I wondered what was going on. And I wasn't alone in that. All eyes were on the doorway without further pretence. There was an underlying silence that even defeated the constant sound of jets. It was peculiar because there was noise all around but everyone involved in this drama, I was convinced, heard nothing, was aware of nothing but the tortuous passing of time and the blank gap of doorway.

There was more background movement in the shadowy entrance. And then they came. Chapman first. Unhurried, he stepped on to the platform and gazed about him with that awkward movement of his head as if he had arrived in some strange country and was taking stock. He was wearing his wisp of beard, his good suit with a Gannex thrown over the shoulders like an actor posing for the press. With his new hairstyle and beard he was recognizable as Chapman only because I had seen him over these past days but there was no semblance to his newspaper photographs.

The two coppers hunched behind him without pushing him on, letting him enjoy his last glimpse of freedom. To give Chapman his due, with capture he had regained his pride. He stood aloof, head high, and it must have cost him much effort. A politician until the last he intended to go out with dignity and the coppers didn't try to deprive him of it.

He stepped forward and his head momentarily lowered as his hand reached for the rail. He never made the first stair. There was a whiplash of sound above, behind, somewhere around me, very faint above the jet noises, and Chapman was thrown back, grabbing his chest as if knifing himself. The two coppers caught him, tried to keep him upright, then one of them tore off the Gannex and they gently lowered him to the platform.

Seconds passed before anything happened. Everyone was stunned, all concentration on the stricken figure. Only gradually did reflexes churn into action because they had all been caught on one leg. The coppers nearest to me began to turn their surprised faces, peering my way while they searched for the possible direction of the shot. I joined them, gazing up at the building, at the windows, at the roof. Some of them had probably not even heard the shot. But common sense told those who had that it must have been a rifle to be so accurate and I wasn't carrying one. They would remember me though.

As one came near I bawled at him, 'There's a way through here up to the offices.' He gave me a look and raced through, followed by another. In the distance some were belting away into walkie-talkies trying to seal off the other side of the airport but I reckon they had a job on. Another copper dashed into the alley and I joined him. As we ran through the Air India office the whole staff was on its feet, bewildered by the sudden flow of traffic. Suddenly I realized I was doing the wrong thing if they were flinging a cordon round; police cars were already pulling up so I retraced my steps and went back airside. The cordon there had disintegrated, vehicles and men racing round the building, for to escape effectively the assassin had to reach the other side.

So I came slowly round the main warehouse block, making my way down towards the break in the cargo tunnel where the road intersected. There was a fair amount of movement all around now as airline staff began to realize that something was drastically wrong. For the moment it helped and police movement was towards the south side of number three terminal.

I wanted to run as far away from the place as possible. With so many coppers around there was always a chance that one of them might recognize me. But I made myself walk slowly, hands in pockets, wondering who the hell had shot poor old Chapman. A siren howled as an ambulance raced to the stationary Boeing.

Reaching the base of the building, I stopped. Ahead of me was the road across the tunnel gap. Obliquely to my left were the open gates with the guard. Normally facing the other way, he kept glancing back because he had probably heard something of the commotion and the howling ambulance. Then a truck approached his side and he had to attend to it, enabling me to slip towards the tunnel.

Crossing the road as near to the right-hand tunnel entrance as possible, because I knew it was a blind spot with the guard, I began my journey towards the edge of the perimeter. I didn't get far. Tucked just inside the tunnel entrance, facing the direction of cargo village, was an Air India van wedged against the tunnel wall.

As soon as I saw it I felt sick. At every turn I was being outwitted. I knew what I would find but I had to see for myself. Creeping alongside the wall I approached the back of the van, putting my ear to one of the rear doors. Hearing nothing I pulled out a handkerchief and opened up. There were parcels in a state of chaos as if someone had pulled out the bottom one and the rest had fallen all over the place.

Time was against me because I couldn't understand why the TV scanners hadn't raised the alarm when the van failed to appear in the second part of the tunnel. I suppose the van was at liberty to branch out of the tunnel and up the intersection but if that were so the system seemed weak. With the concentration of security sealing off the passenger outlets it could be that there was difficulty in detaching someone. But as I crept to the front of the van I still reckoned I was using borrowed time. The offside door was open. My stomach churned until I tasted bile as I saw the two hunched figures inside. The driver had no marks on him and had probably been scientifically coshed. The fellow nearest me was a different sight. He was a middle-aged, smartly dressed Indian with his dark head lolling against the driver's shoulder. Blood was slowly flowing down his face from the jet-black hair; where it reached the obstruction of his thick moustaches it spread out to get through to the chin, slowly dripping from the whiskers. He looked bad and his breathing was shallow.

With my record I didn't fancy being caught beside these two; nor did I like the idea of leaving them. There was nothing that would satisfactorily explain my presence here and I couldn't believe that the alarm hadn't been raised. I got out quick. I could always ring for an ambulance from a safe place if ever I reached one.

I was shaken as I came back on to the road. Everything I had worked out had proved hopelessly wrong. I was out of my league; this was more devious than even Fairfax's connivances – I think. And I didn't like the sight of all that blood.

Right or wrong, I broke into a jog-trot along the perimeter road. It was lucky that the fuzz had been pulled away from this direction or I would have been nicked. When I heard a siren behind me I kept going without looking back. There was no point, and no cover on this open road with the concrete desert on my right. I was heading for the van, of course, anything to get away from this place.

Up the curve of the road the warehouses loomed and near the blind end of the Air India shed I saw one of their little security cars parked and I thought, Oh God, they're waiting. There was some sort of movement in the car park across the road but I was beyond caring. I couldn't go back. Briefly I considered making a dash for the Rising Sun but it didn't seem far enough away from trouble to me and I couldn't know how far the cordon might spread.

So I crossed the perimeter road to the other side of the double yellow lines with no feeling of safety now that I was technically outside the airport. Nearing the car park I slowed considerably because I could now hear movement. The rear of the grey van was visible and the noise seemed to come from its front. Dropping into my noiseless routine, I came slowly up to the van. I took cover behind the nearest car and watched.

The van's bonnet was up and one of Reisen's men known as Moggie Morgan was bending over the engine. In front of the van a very angry Knocker Roberts was removing silver foil from a packet of cigarettes. I realized what he was at. They had expected to find me waiting to drive off. Now they were stuck with no keys and were trying to connect the fuses. The sound of police sirens airside didn't help Knocker's fumbling fingers and he spat out, 'I'll kill the bastard, my God I will.' And I could see that light in his eyes supporting what he had said.

They *would* kill me for this. Did I run or brazen it out? If I ran one day they'd find me. That was a certainty. And it wasn't going to be a tea party if I didn't.

Backing off a little I came running round the side of the car towards the van, panting as if I'd been running all the way. Knocker looked up with red eyes and Moggie hit his head on the raised bonnet as he jerked up in a panic.

'Where the bloody hell have you been, you stupid bastard?' Knocker had a lot of trouble getting his words out.

'Where the hell do you think I've been?' I flared back at him, banging down the bonnet and climbing into the driver's seat. Knocker climbed in beside me, still fuming, ready to throttle me, so I flung out before he could say more, 'How many hours did you expect me to stay there without nature taking a hand? What a cock-up! You call this organization, leaving your driver out on a limb all bloody afternoon?'

'The plane was late in,' he snarled back at me.

Hearing Moggie close the doors behind him at the back, I circled out and drove away from the passenger buildings and the cry of sirens. Knocker was simmering beside me and I played it as if I felt the same so that both of us had a grievance about being let down. The best thing I could do was to give him time to cool: for when Knocker was really angry like now he was as dangerous as an experimental detonator. I didn't know Knocker's explosion point, no one did. So I cooled it and drove well to let him see I was worth waiting for and I thought it strange that he had said the aircraft was late *in* when Reisen had indicated that the snatch was something about to go to the States.

I realized the Air India van was no coincidence. It had been heading towards cargo village after picking up freight from a plane. Suddenly I understood; Chapman wasn't the key but the foil. His plane loaded at roughly the same time as the incoming flight was unloading. Chapman had been betrayed to draw a concentration of security to one point and away from another. And it had worked only too well, except that the incoming flight from Delhi had been late and created an extra problem. But Reisen had sold a beautiful dummy. Anyway, that's the way I saw it. But as I hadn't been too accurate so far I didn't give it too much credence as Knocker told me to head towards Uxbridge. One thing that worried me a lot was Chapman's presumed assassination. It wasn't Reisen's style – not like that in the open; back alleys, dark rivers, acid baths, OK, but public execution?

Then I got round to wondering what I was carrying in the back besides Moggie Morgan. It was impossible for me to look round without rousing Knocker so I quelled my curiosity.

I had been heading south and had turned right on to the A30 to take us westwards. The quickest way to Uxbridge would be to double back and cross the A4 heading towards Drayton, but that would take us past the north and most active side of the airport. So I kept going past Feltham, past the two huge reservoirs that slide under the wheels just before the planes touch down, and into Staines. It was long-winded but safe, and Knocker's lack of comment seemed to endorse my opinion.

At Staines we turned right towards Windsor Great Park, although it was doubtful that the Castle would turn out to be a useful bolthole. We were not out of danger yet. We were still much too near to the airport and there was no telling what police action had been taken. Someone must have found the Air India van by now. I felt a bit easier when we reached the industrial sprawl of Slough and but for odd police spot-checks I reckoned we were now reasonably safe as there was no reason to believe that the van was being sought.

When I stole a quick glance at Knocker I could see that he thought so too. His features were just a shade less aggressive, although for once drawing the better side of face didn't seem to have done much good. Waiting until we slipped on to the suburban scattering of the A4007 on the approaches to Uxbridge I said, 'I'm sorry, Knocker. But I'd given the whole thing up long ago. When I'm working alone I'm on a much tighter schedule. Anyway, I wasn't away long.'

'Long enough, whack. You could have buggered the whole operation.'

He was still angry but he'd called me whack; he was healing.

The traffic was increasing rapidly; we had hit the rush hour. From the corner of my eye I could see that Knocker was slowly losing steam.

As we turned on to the main Uxbridge road I asked, 'Where now?'

'Head for the A40, whack. Oxford direction.'

The traffic wouldn't be much lighter there but it would be faster moving.

'What happened?' I asked slyly.

'What d'yer mean, what happened?'

'At the airport.' I was keeping my gaze firmly in front. 'How did it go?'

'We're bloody here, ain't we, whack? It went fine.'

'Yes, but how did you get to the van? You must have been carrying you know what.'

'I know what but you don't. Stop fishing, you crafty bastard.' But Knocker was grinning, the tension gone, humour back. 'We grabbed one of those security cars and dumped it just opposite the car park.'

That must have been the Air India car I saw near the wall.

'Is that all you'll tell me?' I asked aggrieved.

'That's it, whack.'

'Christ, I can read about it in the evening or morning papers.'

Knocker relented a little. 'The old tricks are the best. Bloke lying in the tunnel, tomato ketchup all over his face and clothes. Terrible sight. Van comes along; it has to stop or run over the body. It stops, driver gets out to examine matey and finds himself looking into the wrong end of a .45. Drivers aren't paid enough to be heroes, so he does exactly what he's told for fear of having his head blown off. He crouches over body as the security car comes up behind the van. Security officer sees van driver bending over bloodied body and comes forward to help. It was too bloody easy. We had some of the boys waiting outside the tunnel to make it nice and quick. We got what we wanted and drove over here in the car.'

'What happened to the van driver and security officer?' He might think it strange if I showed no concern.

'Be your age, whack. We gave them a lump of sugar, patted their heads and sent them home.' Knocker laughed unpleasantly at the recent memory. I didn't need telling who had used the cosh; that would have been the highlight to Knocker. Suddenly he told me to pull up. We were on the outskirts of Uxbridge. Finding a space between parked cars I slipped in, pulled up and kept the engine running.

'OK, Moggie. Out.' Knocker half-turned in his seat.

Moggie had obviously been expecting it for all he complained about was not being dropped near to a bus stop. Knocker slid back his door and went round to open the rear doors. It was my chance to examine the cargo. I was disappointed. All I could see was a sizeable bundle covered with oilskin and tied up with rope. There was a label but I couldn't read it. On Reisen's reckoning that scraggy bundle was worth two million quid. I began to have a horrible insight of what it might be.

Knocker climbed back in and I drove off, keeping the speed moderate. 'Better not shake it up, it might break.'

But Knocker was too crafty. He grinned at me like a wire sponge being squeezed. 'Cunning sod,' he observed mildly. It seemed that he had forgiven me.

Just before we reached the roundabout junction of the A40 he said, 'OK. Pull up, whack.'

I thought quickly. I somehow didn't think we had arrived. This was no area for parked cars but there were two, a Morris 1100 and a Ford Anglia with a fair distance separating them. Gliding in between them I pulled up.

'Out you go,' instructed Knocker.

'Come off it! Where's my food and water? This is the middle of the desert.'

'Sorry, whack. Out.'

'To hell with it. How am I supposed to get back? You could have let me drop off with Moggie.'

'Don't argue, Spider. Find the nearest Green Line stop.'

'I take a bloody dim view,' I complained. But I climbed out.

Knocker was laughing quietly as he moved across to the driver's seat. 'You shouldn't, whack,' he said. 'Not with the amount you're being paid for a piddling drive into the country.' He stuck his head out and sat looking at me. Then he put her in gear and suggested with a baited grin, 'Thumb a lift, whack. See you.'

He drew away and I stepped on to the pavement. So they weren't trusting anyone. My driving skills had been needed for emergencies; now it was safe. The bundle had to be what I thought it was with that much security. No wonder Reisen never did porridge.

The Morris was parked outside a house which lay well back and was obscured by a tall laurel hedge. It was my best bet. I thumped at the louvre window until it loosened, then slid my nail file through to undo the catch. Shoving my arm through I unlocked the door, unfastened the bonnet catch and used my crocodile clip between the fuses. She started immediately. The operation couldn't have taken me a couple of minutes but I had done it in broad daylight on a busy road and I needed my head tested.

Even two minutes is a lot to catch up on so I wasted no time in slipping into the traffic stream after Knocker.

CHAPTER 10

I took the roundabout in a gliding skid. On the A40 I slammed into the outside lane, driving as fast as I could. The truth was I didn't know which turning Knocker had taken off the roundabout. For all I knew mentioning the A40 might have been a blind and he might have been heading back to the Smoke.

I broke a good many laws, changing lanes and passing where I could, but I had to take chances if I was to find Knocker. Traffic was moving well but there was still a lot of it. I could see no sign of the grey van.

Reaching the filter lane for Watford I had to make up my mind whether to take it or carry straight on on the Oxford road. It was a mental toss of the coin. Snarling up the traffic once more I did a quick flip into the left-hand lane and remained on the Oxford road. By constantly using my mirrors I kept my scanners going for Old Bill. By now it was about half-past seven and still light, which was a good thing or I might have given up.

I wasn't doing any blind jobs for Reisen; I wanted to know what I was in. In fact, I almost missed Knocker. I'd been battering away on the fast lane, peering ahead trying to see through the cars in front of me, when the grey smudge appeared in the slow lane to my left. It was awkward because I was coming up on him so fast that it would look odd to suddenly slow and change lanes. Knocker knew how to use wing mirrors as I did.

So I went past him and swung over when I had lost sight of him over a rise in the road. Cursing myself for not being more vigilant I brought my speed down to a crawl but by now there must have been at least a dozen cars between the two of us. I slowed and one by one, with a mixture of British placidity and British aggression, the intervening cars had to pull out and pass me.

Knocker finally appeared like a grey slug two or three cars back. Meanwhile the others overtook me until Knocker was sitting right on my tail. I wanted him in front of me but he seemed in no hurry and in my mirror I could see his gnarled-up face with a half-smoked cigarette drooping from his vice of a mouth. I hoped he hadn't recognized the shape of my head.

I'd been willing him to pass for what seemed hours before he flipped his right-hand indicator, just as I was losing faith in silent communication. But he didn't pass. He drew alongside and I thought he was going to recognize me; he had only to turn his head. What made it worse was that I couldn't keep my eye on him in case he felt the concentration and glanced across. Braking very slowly I let him creep in front. The traffic lights were just ahead and I would have to move over soon in order to follow him. Yet I dared not draw up immediately behind for he was certain to recognize me in his mirror.

Knocker moved forward but was slowing because the lights were red for the right-hand lane only. Shoving my blinker I started to pull out because I could delay no longer. Straddling the lanes I managed to keep on Knocker's blind side. He was about half a length ahead of me with a blue Vauxhall Victor on his tail. If I could ease in behind the Vauxhall I'd be satisfied.

It wasn't to be. Thinking I was in difficulty the bloke in the Vauxhall drew back to let me in. I could have thumped him. Glancing back I saw he was smiling at me, flashing his lights to make sure I'd seen and thereby attracting Knocker. Any other time he would have been hooting me off the road. I drew in behind Knocker, trying to keep away from the focus of his mirror.

As we all stopped at the lights I reflected that I might just as well climb out of the Morris and settle in beside Knocker. He hadn't turned his head but there would be no need for him to. Leaning towards the passenger seat I fiddled as if I was taking something from the nearside door pocket, hoping it would keep my face away from Knocker's questing eyes which I had briefly seen, but fortunately not met, in his mirror.

The A413 Aylesbury road had a garage on either corner. When the lights changed I turned right behind Knocker, flicked up my left blinker, turned into the nearside garage, circled its pumps and came out the way I had gone in. Provided that Knocker had not already seen me it was a neat move which landed me five cars behind him.

We passed through the old villages of Chalfont St Peter

and Chalfont St Giles with a clear blue sky overhead and a big smooth-skinned orange of a sun slipping down towards the Chiltern Hills.

We were back to the winding bits again, on curving high ground with a green valley dipping away to hills on our left. Approaching Amersham, Knocker took me by surprise and flipped his right indicator just as I was getting ready for an evening's solid drive. Riding over to the right with him I hung back with now only one car separating us. So I crept up close to the car in front of me.

We moved slowly off the main road with Knocker hanging back as if unsure of where to go. Or to watch me.

After a hundred yards he switched on his right-hand blinker again. He pulled up to take the turn and I passed him on the inside, noticing a very steep, narrow climb marked 'Private road' to my right. Knowing the area fairly well I continued on, did a full circle outside the railway station, then crept down again, taking it really slow and searching for the turn Knocker had taken.

I had no sooner turned in than I realized it was about a one-in-three climb so I thumped her into low gear and started climbing on my tail. There were a few houses and bungalows lurking behind hedges. Larch and beech trees canopied the narrow climb as I wondered what I could do when I reached the top of this dead-end road.

I took her up just above stalling speed, keeping my eyes skinned trying to peer through foliage and hoping that I wouldn't meet a car coming down. Drives led off the road in unexpected places but I saw no sign of the van. Near the top of the climb I noticed that a small extension of the road led to three new houses, finishing in a cul-de-sac, and branching to the right was the long gravel drive of a big old house, all hanging tiles and leaded windows. The grey van was parked on the gravel.

I had to act quickly and with precious little choice. Seeing a gap in a long stretch of laurel on my left I swung into it, mercifully finding myself in a short drive leading to a white bungalow. Luckily there was no other car in the drive. I stopped, switched off and waited. As nobody came out to ask what I wanted, I assumed that the owners were out and this was supported by the open doors of an empty garage at the end of the drive.

The big house and the van weren't visible in my mirror but if the van drew out I was bound to see it.

Suddenly there was a flash of movement and a squirrel went past at enormous speed followed by a black-and-tan dog old enough to know better. Someone from the direction of the big house repeatedly called Jik and I supposed they were summoning the dog. I hoped like hell that they didn't come looking for him.

Hearing an engine start up I got my radar going and reckoned it was the van. Tyres on gravel, the creeper's enemy, confirmed it. I heard it reverse and swing round before starting down the hill. Then I saw it go past in my mirror. I waited a short time, climbed out and hugging the laurel reached the crest of the hill, which dropped below me like a ski-run. The van was almost at the bottom with its left blinker on. So Knocker was going back to the A413.

I backed the car out, slipped down the hill, turned left at the bottom and parked her a little way down, then returned to the private road on foot. Reaching the point where I had previously parked the car I took an oblique look at the big house.

There was a substantial gap of rough ground either side of it as if space had been left by builders to erect a couple more houses. Over the left-hand wooded wedge-shaped plot a footpath threaded towards a tall fence. Taking it, I kept my head down and walked between the houses through a gap in the fence where a gate had once hung, to find myself on a little tarmac footpath. I turned left on it. It led to a secondary road.

I had already made up my mind to screw the big house so I was now plotting avenues of escape. If there hadn't been this way out I think I would have given up the idea; I've always been afraid of being trapped in alleys or cul-de-sacs. The job appeared too simple and that made me wary. Now I took the right-hand direction along the tarred footpath behind the fence. It finished up in three branches. The right tributary was a narrow dirt footpath along which the fence continued. So did I. It was a rewarding move. The fence ended and I found myself behind the garden of the big house. It was partly hidden by a line of young beech, honeysuckle and lilac. But by peering through the gaps I was able to get a fairly good view of the house and lawn. Threaded through the saplings just in front of me was stout wire-mesh. It was going to be easier this side.

Just then someone came out and old Jik pranced around yapping for a stone; for an old 'un he had lots of bounce, which worried me a bit for he clearly belonged to the house.

Following the path along, it shelved steeply and came out on to the main road just below where I had parked the car. I drove the Morris back to within five hundred yards of where I had picked it up.

That night I had to nick another car. It was one-thirty A.M. when I swung on to the Aylesbury road again and there was so little traffic that I was able to drive most of the remaining seven miles to Amersham at full speed. I passed the private road and took the next turning on my right. I wasted a lot of time in a series of trial-and-error moves while I searched for the road that led back to the narrow tarred track. I had underestimated the number and combination of turnings from these rural roads, not all of which were lighted.

Eventually I found the path, turned the car round so that I was facing the way I had come, doused to sidelights, then climbed out. Now past two, there was not a house light in sight. Following the fence, I swung right down the footpath until I reached the back of the big house. Creeping up to the wire fence I tested it to find that the right-hand section was hooked to the end of the wooden fence and could be rolled back to reveal a path to the lawn.

I didn't like it this easy; I preferred a few snags to sharpen my senses. At the foot of the lawn I could see the big house looming under trees rising behind it. One window on the upper floor was open so I took it to be a bedroom.

I walked silently over the lawn past a few fruit trees and reached a paved terrace. Facing me was what was obviously the kitchen door and for the rest it was red brick and leaded windows, with all the curtains drawn across so that I couldn't see in. I shone my torch through the glass and detected a window catch halfway down the wooden frame and, at the base of the window, a metal retaining bar. The strength of this house was its innocence; had I not followed Knocker it was as safe a hidey-hole as anywhere could be.

The simplest way of entry was to break one of the small panes and put my arm through, but it was so unearthly quiet that I decided against it. I did it the hard way, bending back the lead section by section with a kind of bottle-opener I have until the small glass pane was ready to drop out. I removed it with a plug of plasticine and quietly laid it down well away from my feet. I was about to open the window when I heard a soft thumping from inside the room that froze me solid. It was like the faint pad of a muffled drum. It made my hair stand on end. Then I thought it must be the wind catching something. I put my arm through and very slowly pulled back one side of the curtain. The thumping was clearer and a little faster.

Risking torchlight I directed the beam into the room and two green orbs caught the light and almost made me drop the torch. The eyes were baleful until I shifted the beam. It was old Jik waiting to greet me, his tail striking excitedly against an armchair. I'd never had trouble with dogs; the danger from this one was not that he would start barking a warning but that he might yap from excitement.

Grinning in the darkness I said hello, put my arm right through, loosened the bar, then undid the catch. When I pushed the window carefully it wouldn't budge. Jik started prancing, with low squeals in the back of his throat as he sensed a new sort of game. I tried to calm him as I found the area of resistance. Running my fingers up inside the frame I located my old friend the Chubb lock. It's easy enough to obtain keys for this type of lock. I pulled out a cylindrical key and inserted it, unscrewed and then pulled back the lock; it was awkward but my main concern was the impatient dog.

Now the window was open I made sure there was nothing directly under the sill, then climbed through. Jik jumped all over me, licking my face as I crouched to him. I had to spend some minutes fussing over him, then calming him down.

I was in the lounge, large and well-furnished, but I quickly established that there was nowhere where the bundle I had seen in the van could be stacked. Two doors either side of a pseudo Adam fireplace were open to give Jik the run of the house.

The left-hand room was a dining-room with a long Regency table and copy Hepplewhite chairs. There was some silver worth nicking but that wasn't why I was here. I went back through the lounge and into a study. Again there was no sign of the bundle.

Two things had contributed to my speed so far; the carpeting throughout had muffled my tread and Jik's gambolling, and the drawn curtains had permitted me free use of the torch. I went through the study into the hall to find the kitchen at the end of it. It took me longer here; there were many cupboards and I examined them all. I even pulled out the washing machine and looked inside it, as well as the fridge and underneath the sink unit. If Knocker had dumped his load here then it wasn't downstairs. It was possible that it had been moved on elsewhere while I had returned to London but now I was in I had to go the whole hog.

Jik had quietened down and I led him back to the lounge and told him to stay. He panted a tacit agreement while I wondered how Reisen could be involved in such a homely setup. It was so cosy it shocked me to realize that if I was caught in this house I would be topped without trial.

I had to take to the stairs. I didn't like it because there must be three or four bedrooms and I'd be within easy earshot of each one. Before going up I eased back two huge bolts on the front door and released the catch on the Yale lock. I might want a quick way out.

Although the stairs were carpeted I knew they would be creakers because of the age of the house. Hugging the wall-side I went up. Jik stayed behind, which was a relief.

The boards were so old and badly nailed that I had to lower my weight gradually on each one before mounting the next. I reached the narrow landing; two doors to my left, one ahead and one on my right. The door immediately on my left bore a pottery plaque which proclaimed it 'The Den'. I decided to try the farthest door first. Putting my ear to it I reckoned the room was empty and went in. The curtains were drawn back which limited the use of the torch but there was just enough light to reveal a large bedroom. There were cupboards and a big wardrobe apart from two beds. About halfway through a fruitless search I heard a board creak on the landing. And then again. It wasn't old wood protesting about the weather; pressure had been put on floorboards. I doused the torch and stood rigid.

After a while I heard it again; faint but unmistakable. Yet I could hear no movement. Creeping to the door I listened with my ear to the wood and could hear a faint padding, then a tiny squeal. As I quietly opened the door I was pushed back by a bundle of fur that slobbered all over me. Jik was proving to be an embarrassment. Back on the landing I held his collar while I listened at another door facing the rear of the house; there was the sound of breathing. The opposite door was partly open and turned out to belong to the bathroom. The only hiding-places there were the airing cupboard and the bath. I began to think I was wrong.

Because of Jik, who had decided not to leave me, I took the Den next, leaving the occupied room as a last desperate measure. Still I stopped to listen at the door before entering. Jik nipped in with me and I closed the door behind us as I didn't want him prancing on the loose boards on the landing.

It was a small, odd-shaped room with, incongruously, a

massive chest deep-freeze along one recessed wall and a desk opposite. There was a short narrow corridor before the room spread out to my left with a bookcase full of *Britannica* at right-angles to the deep-freeze. Jik parked himself in the desk kneehole as if it was a kennel while I looked around. There was little room here and it was at once clear that the desk desk and bookcase could not hold the bundle. The thermostat of the deep-freeze cut out while I stood there and startled both Jik and myself.

Rubbing Jik's head to reassure him I gazed round the gloom of the room, somehow feeling that I was close. I had to be because I didn't fancy my chances in the other bedroom. The freezer would be a good place to hide it. I took the lid handle in both hands and pressed the catch. The bloody thing was locked. Christ! And then I heard a door open across the landing and a heavy tread on the loose boards under the carpeting. I moved back quickly against the bookcase so that if anyone opened the door I would not be seen immediately. Someone went into the bathroom and before I could do a thing about it Jik ran for the door, scratched at it vigorously and yapped.

CHAPTER 11

As I stood there stiff with apprehension I didn't need reminding that this was the Reisens' territory. I whispered to Jik but he had heard one of his masters and his scratching was persistent. A lot of other villains I know would have throttled him but I couldn't do it even to save myself.

There were still noises from the bathroom; running water, then a cistern filling and humming water pipes. Jik yapped again, then I heard a woman from the bedroom call out, 'Fred, is that Jik up here?'

Fred stopped moving about to listen and Jik scratched and

yapped again on cue. There was complete silence outside while I tried to push myself through the bookcase wall.

The woman yelled, 'He's in the Den. How did he get in there?'

Fred, feeling the accusation, said nothing but opened the door. I heard Jik pound out and leap up at his master with his little squeals of delight, then the light came on and I thought this was it. There was the sound of a footfall in the short corridor and I knew that Fred was looking into the room.

The woman called out, 'Poor little devil. Come here, son. Come to mummy.' Then more loudly, 'You locked him in there, you careless pig. Fancy locking him in.'

Fred's aggrieved voice was much too close for comfort.

'I didn't. I didn't see him. He must have been under the desk. Anyway, he was downstairs when we came to bed.'

'You said he was. Selfish pig. He must have followed you up when you checked the freezer. Fancy not noticing. Come on, son, you stay with us for the rest of the night.'

Fred, quietly swearing to himself, was just about to step into the room, I even saw part of his face emerge, when the woman called out again. 'Come on, get him some water, he's panting his head off. And come and say you're sorry to him.'

Fred swore loudly, switching off the light and slamming the door behind him. I could hear a muffled argument, with the woman's voice prominent. For some seconds I couldn't move. It doesn't matter how experienced you are, a sudden danger sends the sweat flowing and increases the adrenalin. You never get used to it, just a shade wiser, that's all. I had remained completely still and had somehow controlled my breathing; that and the woman's aggressiveness had saved me.

The bedroom door slammed and the arguing diminished to a murmur. It was safe to move. I sat down in a repro-period chair at the repro desk and sent up a little prayer of gratitude and waited a minute or two for my senses to revert to normal.

So the freezer was locked. I opened the middle drawer of

the desk and there in the near corner were two small flat keys on a split ring. My luck was running sweetly.

I unlocked the deep-freeze and as I lifted the lid the interior light came on. I hoped there was no one outside to see. Four plastic baskets contained a variety of frozen vegetables, potted shrimps and paté. Lifting out two baskets I gazed at the package. It occupied most of the interior, its oilskin covering already sparkling with frost.

I stood looking down. To be sure of its contents I would have to cut the covering and that was virtually leaving a visiting card. There was no time to untie frozen knots and anyway I would never get it back the same. So I had to rest content. Putting back the trays I closed the lid, locked it, replaced the keys, then put my ear to the door. They had quietened down in the bedroom but that was no guarantee of sleep. I returned to the desk and decided to give it half an hour on the basis that it takes the average person twenty minutes to fall asleep. An angry mind like Fred's would take longer.

Filling in time by going through the desk produced nothing but innocent correspondence. Even villains get involved with rates and insurance and sometimes with tax.

I moved, opening the door slowly. I was scared now because I knew that the sensitive ears of Jik would hear me. Would he respond? I didn't wait too long to find out and went down the stairs faster than I should. There was no disturbance from above so maybe Jik had called it a day.

Normally that would have been it. But in this case I had to be sure that no one would know that I had been here. I re-locked and bolted the front door and then, outside the house, sat on my nerves and replaced the pane of glass. It wasn't easy to get it back as I'd found it but I hoped that it was near enough. Nor had I forgotten to screw up the burglar lock. As I trundled down the lawn I reflected that I had just committed the perfect job, nothing taken; no signs of entry. But I wasn't really kidding myself, there's no such thing as the perfect job.

The next morning the papers had a field day. The Chapman shooting overrode everything else. And Chapman was dead. He had died as soon as the bullet struck him, which was the best that could be said. Who had killed him? And why? The papers screamed the questions and came up with every conceivable answer so that they could quote themselves at a later date to show how clever they were. I couldn't help wondering if the person he had died for was worth it.

But the shooting wasn't news to me; I had witnessed it. What *was* news I found inside. It might have been front page on its own account but for Chapman. As it was it was almost tucked away and occupied only half a column under a sub-heading : Opium Snatch. I read on without surprise. Apparently it was a regular delivery of opium for Boots the Chemists who used it for drugs and opiates. The only difference between this delivery and others was that it was an accumulation of three shipments which had been held up by a strike in Delhi.

And I knew where it was. It was highly dangerous knowledge. Reisen wasn't kidding when he had intimated that the snatch was worth two million quid. So much opium was worth easily that by the time the boys had processed it to heroin and diluted it. And hundreds of kids would begin the slow death, the no-way back route to craving disaster. Slow murder.

I decided to break my own golden rule. I did it with great reluctance but no less inevitably; there was no other course. I went to the nearest phone booth, placed a handkerchief over the mouthpiece and rang New Scotland Yard, asking for someone in the drug squad.

Of all the things I've done this was the strangest of my life. Spider Scott grassing. I had a nasty taste in my mouth and was so disturbed that I hung up before I was put through. I wiped my forehead and leaned against the side of the kiosk. I felt as Judas must have felt. All right; Reisen and his mob were murdering bastards but I had lived in part of their world, the line beyond the law. Why did I have to be the Charlie to put the finger on them? Why was I doing it anyway? Because they had lied to me? Taken me for a sucker? It was none of this; I had done my own share of deceiving them. Simply it was drugs. It was the one thing most villains and me in particular abhorred.

All this went through my head as I sweated it out in the phone booth. The actual act of grassing had forced me to find an excuse not to. And in the end I came up with no real answer. I only knew that I couldn't allow Reisen to spread this particular brand of evil. I picked up the receiver again and this time went through with it, listening to a voice that wasn't mine and leaving the booth as if I had just received an overdose myself.

Outside, I walked without seeing. I don't expect the layman to understand but I felt treacherous. Yet for all my qualms I knew that I had done the right thing; the only thing. But I got no comfort from it. At least I hadn't cashed in on the knowledge; there was no profit in it for me and financially I had lost a good deal. I just hoped that Reisen never got an inkling that it was me.

At the office they all looked up in some wonderment at my appearance. I suppose the staff had been hoping that I would stay away permanently so they could get on with it. So I growled about the place to let them know that I was still boss, asked a lot of damned silly questions to keep them aware that I was as sharp as ever, and then I let them continue running things. Smoky Joe brought me a cup of coffee in between delivering tickets and Lulu gave me a look as if I'd been scrounging round dustbins all night.

I looked at the paper. The assassination of Chapman had caused a bigger stir and bigger banners than his treason and disappearance had done.

The security services came heavily under the hammer for bungling and the police took a caning for letting the assassin slip through their cordon. The front page contained little else. Inside was an obituary which never reached the heart of the man I had known so briefly. Poor Chapman; even now he'd gone they couldn't leave him alone.

Just before lunch, on inspiration, I rang the Soviet Embassy. I asked for Colonel Kransouski. This shook them as the Colonel is head of their espionage network in this country. The bloke the other end of the wire became confused and suspicious and both showed. 'Tell him it's Spider,' I said. 'He'll know.'

There was a good long pause and then the Colonel came on as smooth as Polish vodka. 'Mr Scott? How delighted I am to hear from you. What can I possibly do to help you?'

The suave bastard sounded in good form. The last time we had met he had blackmailed me and then had his strong-arm man Fido knock the daylights out of me. But there was something between us. 'Knocked anybody off lately?' I asked him jovially. 'Didn't expect to find you in. Thought you might be out stirring up the Unions or the Free Welsh, or someone.'

He wasn't devoid of humour. 'As you discovered, we do not knock people off, Mr Scott. We may bluff just a little, eh? Like good chess men. But I am sure you would not ring me up just to call me names.'

'Thought you might want to buy me a lunch. Have a chat.'

'About what?' He was all there, was Boris. I could feel him scrabbling down the line at me.

'Knocking people off. Alan Bruce Chapman for instance.'

'Ah! You know something?'

'Nothing. And you?'

'Nothing. Tragic business.'

'Well, shall we meet to discuss what we both don't know?' Boris would not believe that I knew nothing, it would be foreign to his nature.

'Why not? I will be delighted to see you. Can you be here by one?'

I laughed. Boris never gave up trying. 'I'm not setting foot in that place; I've had my fill of embassies.'

We met in a small exclusive restaurant in St John's Wood. Boris was dressed in his traditional grey, but lightweight as it was spring and he carried a grey trilby in his hand. His good-looking, lined face vaguely creased into a smile as we met. He offered his hand and I thought, what the hell, so I shook it. Anyway, he was paying. His manner was quite different from the last time we met. He was more guarded in the knowledge that I had beaten him and he showed proper respect. But I wasn't underestimating him. If Boris ever had a chance to even things up he would delight in every moment of it.

'Why do you always wear grey?' I asked. 'To match your eyes and hair?'

'No, your weather, Mr Scott. Sackcloth and ashes. I am in a state of semi-mourning at the terrible dampness of your country.'

We were well into the main course when he said, 'Now what of Chapman?'

'I was hoping you'd tell me. I wondered why you had knocked him off?'

He stared at me quietly for a moment. I went cold as his gaze reached me. All bantering had gone.

'It is incredibly clumsy of Sir Stuart Halliman to send you as emissary in an effort to hide your own guilt. We had every reason to keep Chapman alive. Whereas you had every reason to want him dead, wouldn't you say?'

Like everyone else, Boris would not believe that I didn't work for DI5 and he had more reason to believe it than most. No denial from me would change his opinion and there were advantages in playing along with it. 'You know we don't do that sort of thing.'

He smiled thinly. 'You reflect your master, which is a pity. I have not found you a hypocrite before.'

I'd been kidding but I let it pass. 'It wasn't *us*,' I rejoined. 'Or I wouldn't be here now.'

'You find it necessary to reassure me?' He sipped his wine expertly, seeking the reason for my being here. It wouldn't dawn on him that I was personally interested and also involved in a way far from his conjectures.

'No. Our newspapers have done their stuff. No prompting. Free press. All the angles.'

'Oh yes. Of course. Papers full of rubbish. Then why are you here?'

'To see you, Boris, old cocker. Well, if you didn't do it and we didn't do it, who did?'

'I do not accept for one moment that you did not. It was very convenient for you, was it not? Much more convenient than sending him back to prison where we might have introduced a contact.'

'I didn't think you went in for that stuff. Dear me. Well, then, what about this? You paid some villains to spring Chapman and the Chinese knocked him off because they couldn't have him.'

He shrugged. He had not dismissed the idea, but he didn't go a bundle on it either. As he didn't reply I said, 'Suppose the villains took your money to spring him then found another use for him, like making an opium snatch while all attention was on Chapman. Supposing they used him this way but never had any intention of actually letting him go to Russia. But they had to make it look as if they'd earned their money.'

Boris put on his mask of urbanity. He was really good at it. His fingers delicately handled his cutlery and his jaw clamped slowly, almost imperceptibly as he continued to enjoy his fillet steak with fried egg. He knew his spies, his agents, his traitors, his weaklings, but I would gamble that he did not know his villains. They were in another dimension. To Boris they would be thieves, thugs, dishonest right through, money their God. And he would be right up to a point. But *I* knew them and he took note of what I said. It was impossible to judge how the idea took him but from his continued, measured silence I could tell that I had struck a weak spot. I don't think that he had considered the possibility. When he fell back on the old party denial line I knew for certain that I had him worried. It would hit Boris hard to discover that he had been taken for a sucker by a bunch of villains.

'I resent your inference,' he said coldly, 'that we would employ bandits to release a man like Chapman. There would be no need. It's a monstrous suggestion, Mr Scott.'

So he had gone dignified on me. But it was as good as a confession.

I saw Penny that evening at her mews cottage. She seemed surprised to see me. She led me in and we embraced like parting lovers instead of with the evening stretching ahead of us.

'I needed that,' she panted as she finally broke away. 'I've missed you, Willie. I thought you were coming last night.'

She was wearing a black silk slip of a thing which reached mid-thigh length and there was a hungry passion in her gaze as if she was afraid I would disappear and wanted satisfaction before I did. She had an eagerness and an intensity that was new. She hadn't lacked passion before but this was as if she knew that there was only one bite left of the forbidden fruit. I wasn't complaining; it was the right remedy after a day of tension. We finished up on the sofa and it was a long time before we got round to questions. We weren't burned out yet; just resting between rounds. Penny brought in coffee to build up our strength.

'What time *did* you get back after that job yesterday?' she asked.

Careful, Spider. 'Oh, I don't know. Ninish. Knocker dropped me off in the middle of the desert and I had trouble getting back. I was clapped out.'

'I bet you were.'

I looked across for the hidden meaning but those hazel eyes were teasing me in a delightful way so I suppose it was my guilty conscience.

She searched around the cushions and finally found an evening paper which she tossed across to me. 'Have you seen this?'

The front page was still on Chapman. An old American Army Springfield rifle with telescopic sights had been found in a broom cupboard near one of the offices in Number Three Building at London Airport. The number had been filed off and there were no other identifying marks; which meant the killer had worn gloves and they hadn't a clue who the gun belonged to.

'He got what he deserved,' I said, feeling a hypocrite and recalling her earlier views on the subject.

'Yes, he did. But I didn't mean that. The centre pages.'

I gave her a curious look but she was hiding behind the old expression which had always puzzled me. Still, I opened the paper, lifting it so that it hid my face. It was a wise precaution. The headline read : Opium Recovered : a man and a woman are helping the police with their inquiries. Feeling my blood mounting, I knew that I was walking the old eggshells again.

'This bit about the opium?' I called through the paper.

'Yes.'

'What about it?'

'Well, haven't you read it? Read it all.'

So I did, slowly, wondering what I should say. And so would she be. The police had raided the house in Amersham about midday. They must have moved fast after my phone call. It mentioned that the stuff had been snatched from London Airport the previous day. Lowering the paper I stared at her in what I hoped was disbelief. 'You mean to say that this was the job I was on?'

'Well, don't you know?' She eyed me curiously.

'How the hell should I? I wasn't told what we were snatching.'

'Weren't you curious?'

'Of course I was bloody curious. It didn't get me anywhere. I don't like it. I've never dealt in drugs.' I rose, screwing up the paper and throwing it into the chair.

'Sit down and finish your coffee, Willie.'

'I've suddenly gone off it.' Passion was now a long way away. It would be out of character for me not to protest against the drugs but it carried certain dangers.

'Someone has grassed, you realize that?' Penny flung at me.

'Unless Knocker was careless.'

'He wasn't careless enough to take you all the way. Did you know he was going to Amersham?'

'How could I? We were on the Oxford road, but it could have been anywhere out there. To tell the truth, I thought he was going to double back.'

'So you thought about it.'

I stared down at her. 'What are you getting at? Of course I thought about it. I thought about it a lot but there wasn't much I could do about it.'

'You could have nicked a car and followed him.'

'Oh, yes. I'm the great boy for sticking his neck out and getting it chopped off. What are you suggesting?'

'Look, Willie. Reisen is going to look for a head. He's just lost a fortune in opium apart from the running costs of the snatch. He has to pay the boys. The two the police are holding wouldn't have grassed against themselves so it leaves a very limited choice. And you must be high on the list.'

'You said it yourself, I'm the great non-grasser. Why talk like this?'

She stood in front of me and took my hands, making a ball of them inside hers. 'I'm trying to help you. Supposing Reisen has heard a rumble about me wanting to leave him. He knows we meet. Suppose he reasons that I might try a break and that you might threaten to finger him for the opium snatch as a kind of insurance to keep him away from me. He might think you've done a deal with the insurance people to get a cash return.'

'Penny, for goodness sake, I stood to make over twenty grand.'

'Yes, but would you have taken it once you knew that the money came from drugs?'

I stared at her. It was a good question. 'No, I wouldn't,' I admitted.

'And don't you think Reisen would know that? Oh, Willie, why do you think he kept it so secret from you?'

That I could see. What I had not understood all along was why he had troubled with me at all. There was no sense in it to me, but there had to be to Reisen.

I went to the office early the next morning. I was beginning to worry the staff for they were finding me unpredictable and staff like their bosses to have regular habits. I checked that Reisen's boys were still booking with us, then got down to the job of learning something of the travel business. Smoky Joe was trotting around town collecting passports and visas and delivering tickets; it wasn't much of a job but he could have time off to look for another and it at least kept him out of trouble. It was a pity I didn't follow the same simple rules. I was worried because Penny knew better than most how Reisen ticked, and I didn't like her chain of thought.

When Smoky Joe brought in the morning coffee he hovered around my desk like he was barefooted on hot coals. 'What's the matter?' I asked glancing up.

'Can I have a word with you, boss?'

'Of course.' I thought he looked scared.

He rolled his eyes in the direction of the two girls thumping typewriters and said, 'It's sort of private.'

Thinking it was trouble with his wife and kids which he didn't want the girls to hear about, I got up. 'Let's go outside.'

We went out into the street, the most private place to talk. Standing with my back to our own shop window I said, 'Out with it.'

But Smoky was scared. He was still shuffling on cinders and I said, 'Come on, Smoky.'

'I hear the finger's on you, boss.'

'Finger? What are you talking about?'

'Reisen's after you. He's going to top you for sure.'

'When did you hear this?' I made it casual but my skin was crawling.

'Round and about. You know how it is. But it's for sure. I thought you better know.'

It wasn't fair to press him further and it wouldn't have got me anywhere. If Reisen was after me then Reisen would get me – eventually – whatever I did.

'OK, Smoky. Thanks for the tip. Do you know when he's moving in?'

'Nope. An' ah'm not likely to hear.'

'Leave it with me. You go inside.' I went and sat on one of the wooden benches in Trafalgar Square. With the fountain playing and the visitors out to catch the spring sun it seemed crazy to nurse the sort of thoughts that churned round in my head. One way or another Reisen had been after me from the outset. Trying to fix me was one thing; topping me was quite another. And he'd kill me the slow way; there was no compassion with Reisen.

CHAPTER 12

It would be easy for him to keep tabs on me from the office although I didn't think he would try anything in daylight. As I tried to work out what to do and lunchtime came and passed light became very precious. I cleared up at the office, checked with young Charlie Hewitt that everything was under control, then hinted to him that I might not be in for a day or two. It was difficult to judge whether his look was of restrained relief or dutiful concern.

I left the office and went through the routine of shaking off limpets. In fact I don't think I was followed; Reisen didn't have to worry about time and he knew that I hadn't the funds to go to earth for long. That was the terrible thing about it, there was no safety in time; part of the punishment could be sweating it out awaiting Reisen's pleasure.

There was one place where he would not look for me at this time of day. I went to Penny's mews cottage and let myself in; it took no longer than using a key. I took off my jacket and put my legs up on the settee, determined to get what comfort I could.

I had no ready money. Which meant a return to crime and eventual recognition by the local criminal fraternity, which in turn meant that Reisen would hear of me because his contacts were enormous. Anyway, I wouldn't leave my own patch.

It was a long wait even though I knew when I could expect Penny. When you see part reason for a thing but can't get to the real core, the point that really makes it all stand up, then you slowly drive yourself mad.

The sound of the key in the lock jolted me. I had left the lounge door open so that I would hear clearly. It was just before seven. There were the usual noises around the cloak cupboard. The faint pad of her tread was clear, then suddenly it wasn't and I knew that she had flipped off her shoes. She came softly in, a newspaper tucked under one fair-skinned arm which emerged from a white silk sleeveless blouse. She stopped when she saw me : the paper dropped to the floor and her reaction was not what I expected.

Her first expression, understandably, was one of alarm as she saw a man when the place should have been empty. Certainly I would have finally expected her to be pleased, even if she had thrown something at me in passing. With shock I realized that she was verging on panic. She was not only more deeply alarmed than at first but was backing towards the door.

'It's me, for God's sake.' I was quickly out of the chair. 'Me. Your old lovey dovey, Spider.' I approached slowly because she was on the point of running. 'Penny, what's the matter?'

She was fighting the panic and her expression calmed a fraction. Like this I didn't even know her. I'd laid something bare that I'd rather not have seen. Then she fought back a little harder and stopped retreating from me. I began to recognize her when her lips trembled and one hand went to her breast.

'Don't you ever do that to me again, Willie Scott.' She was breathless, her voice subdued and shaky. 'Don't ever come in here again like that.'

I went over to her, put my arms about her but there was no response. She was trembling slightly, yet I felt it couldn't have been that bad a shock. Soothing her, she gradually unwound then clutched me fiercely and I thought she was going to cry but she was too strong for that.

'If I'd known I was going to have that effect on you I wouldn't have done it,' I said gently.

She was coming round quickly. 'Oh, Willie, it wasn't you. You must understand that working for a man like Reisen carries its risks. He has his enemies. I don't want them at me.'

I let it go at that; then, 'I had to drop in like this,' I explained. 'Reisen's after me. He's going to kill me.'

Again she fooled me on reaction. She did her best to look shocked but it was too soon after the first jolt. She stood like a bad actress trying out a pose. My suspicions were born in a numb sort of way. I had caught her flat-footed and she was recovering too slowly.

'You don't seem too concerned,' I said brusquely.

She pulled down the edge of her blouse, a calculated movement but it was too late for all that. 'Oh, don't be silly,' she said. 'I can't take it seriously, that's all.'

'Why? Has Reisen given up topping people?'

She replied faster but I think she was afraid it was too late. Smiling, she approached me with something like her old composure but her eyes were masked behind a hard glaze. She tried to put her arms round my neck but I backed off. Realizing that she'd mugged it she had fallen back on sex to make things worse.

'You know about it,' I accused her, feeling trapped. I had known she was no saint but considered we had an understanding. Self interest I could understand, treachery was another matter.

'Oh, don't be silly, Willie, you're beginning to make me angry.'

'And you're turning my stomach. You know the finger's on me, that's why you were so shaken to see me here. My God! What about our date tonight? What were you going to do? Ring me to call it off or just not be here?'

Her Celtic temper was rising above her other emotions. I had hit her on the raw and her eyes blazed but at least she was now looking straight at me. 'God, you're a child. Do you realize what you're saying? I happen to be very fond of you.' She ran fingers through her hair in a sort of exasperated movement and if she'd been like this at the outset she would have fooled me. 'I should have you thrown right out of here, Willie. Now sit down while I make some coffee and then we'll talk sensibly.'

She went past me, head high, straight-backed, breasts hard against her blouse, then she turned at the door. 'Sit,' she ordered as if I were her pet dog. 'This has all gone wrong but we'll sort it out. It's too bloody ridiculous for words.'

I sat and Penny marched out. I was numb, angry at myself, and cursed my own conceit. But I wasn't completely stupid. She left the door partially open, which was a good honest move, and I made no noise in crossing to it. The sounds of a kettle being filled and crockery being set up reached me clearly; too clearly. By stretching my ears out on trellis I heard another sound and I was round that door as if my life depended on it. She had a tea cosy over the extension phone to muffle her dialling. As I crossed the kitchen in one long stride she went deathly white. I yanked the cord from the wall just as the number started to ring.

'You bloody bitch.'

There was no pretence now, nothing she could say. She still clung to the useless handpiece staring vapidly at the broken cord. Then she tried to hit me over the head with it but I caught her wrist easily, wrenched away the handpiece and pushed her back against the counter top.

'Why, Penny?' I pleaded. 'I've done nothing to you. Why?'

Having no more need to act she became the person I met first time. She leaned against the counter holding the wrist I had twisted and said wearily, 'I'm really very fond of you. I can't expect you to understand.'

'There has to be a reason, so let's have it.'

She was very practical about it. 'If I have to choose between what we have between us and what I possess then the material will win every time. Don't you see, Willie? I have no security, never have had. You can't provide any for me even if you were serious enough and from what I hear I'd never take Maggie Parson's place. So I intend to hang on like grim death to what I have.'

'Even at my expense?'

'I'm sorry, Willie, but it's too plain to me even to constitute a choice. I'm not returning to the gutter – for you or anyone.'

'So this business of wanting to leave Reisen was a load of lies.' I stared angrily, beginning to loathe her. 'He put you up to it.' Advancing on her, it was all I could do to stop myself shaking the life from her. 'Well, didn't he?' I grabbed her arm and she struggled, trying to bite my hand.

'I really did grow fond of you, Willie. Let go for God's sake.'

Standing back I took stock of her. There was no repentance. It didn't matter to her for her priorities were too well defined. Her hair was hanging around her face and she was glaring back at me, one hand searching along the counter top for something she might attack me with. I didn't try to stop her; somehow it didn't matter. What I'd missed but lately seen traces of without it registering, was now as clear as her own rising breasts. It was greed that motivated her; avarice and possession. Everything was secondary to that. She was so busy piling up a monetary barrier between herself and her childhood memories that everything else, no matter how intense the pleasure, was a tributary to it. Moralizing was useless; she was beyond help. She must have seen the pity following on my disgust, for she said, 'You couldn't expect me to put myself in hock for you.'

'No. I don't blame you for hiding behind Reisen when he's your pay-lord. But you could have warned me at some point without damaging yourself. You could have told him I'd run cold and let us both off the hook.'

'I couldn't take that chance.'

'The question now is what am I going to do with you?'

'Willie, I'm sorry. Just walk out and leave me.'

She was not apologizing for what she had done but for a vague recognition of what she was.

'Sit down,' I said.

When she didn't move, I added, 'I've never belted a woman but by God you're tempting me. Now sit down.'

Using the telephone flex, I tied her hands behind the wooden chairback, pulled some more from the wall, the staples flying across the kitchen, then tied her feet. Flex is awkward stuff so it wasn't a proper job but I hoped it would hold her for a bit. I just needed a little time. Making sure that she was secure I went upstairs to her bedroom. Looking through the lace drapes covering the windows I noticed the two lamps set high in the wall opposite like gas lamps in nineteenth-century London. It wasn't yet pitch dark, so I could still see both ends of the mews reasonably well. At the end of the street a man leaned against the wall reading a magazine. At the other end a car was parked with sidelights on : I couldn't see if there was anyone in it; I didn't have to. The man with the magazine took a sly look up the mews and over to Penny's cottage.

So they were waiting for me; not to come out but to go in. And I was late. Running down the stairs I found that Penny had wriggled the chair through the kitchen door and half-way across the lounge. She gave up as I came in. 'You beauty,' I jeered. 'You not only knew but you told Reisen when I was coming. You've put me on the spot, you bitch.' Seeing her position I assumed that she was trying to get near enough to the front door to yell through it. She kept her expression neutral.

Grabbing the chair-back, I dragged her roughly into the kitchen, pulled another stretch of flex from the wall then opened the cupboard of the sink unit. I tied the stave of the chair to the copper piping under the sink. The knots were too low both ends for her to reach.

'There you are,' I said. 'If you want to break away from that you can pull the sink out first.'

'You bastard,' she flung at me. She was getting down to basics, the sophisticated secretary having disappeared com-

letely in an accent that had returned to the Gorbals. Back
upstairs I raided the bathroom medicine cabinet and took
some adhesive tape to cover her mouth.

'You've been conning me from the outset. I'll tell Reisen
you balled it up,' I told her, to make her sweat after I'd
gone. Then I left, having turned the radio on softly just to
cover any noise she might make. In the small courtyard beyond the kitchen I took a pull at the drainpipe and started
up.

It was an awkward roof. I had to flatten myself face
downwards against the tiles with my feet on top of the gutter
and it was slow going. When I reached the buildings that
angled on to the main street I had to climb another stack to
a higher roof level and start the same caper again with a bigger distance to fall. However, I had earmarked an open
window about halfway along with a pipe running near it. I
glanced down periodically to locate the down-pipe hole in
the guttering. In the bad light it was difficult so I had to use
my feet as antennae, feeling my way, groping for the hole.

When I finally found it I was faced with the toughest
problem of all; to get from the roof on to the down-pipe
without breaking my neck. I let my feet dangle over the
edge, keeping flat against the roof and using my hands as
suction pads, hoping that I didn't gather momentum; if I
did the guttering wouldn't save me. The farther I slid over
the edge the more difficult became the suction. It reached a
point where I felt myself going, so I curled my legs under the
eaves and searched for the pipe with my feet. Finding it, my
feet gripped and I transferred my hand grip to the guttering,
hoping it would hold but taking a lot of weight on my feet.
It was a dicey move coming from the roof and under the
eaves to the pipe. It's not the sort of move I like to make
when screwing a drum. Maybe I'm just getting past it, but
the funny thing was, as always on a job, I was enjoying myself.

I made the pipe, then the going was easy until I reached
a tributary running underneath the window I wanted. Resting, I noticed the reflection of lights below me but the open

window was in darkness. Keeping my feet on the tributary I let go of the main pipe to allow my body to fall across towards the window. I grabbed the sill and pulled myself up in one movement. As I came up I shot one hand inside to unlatch the bar and pull the window wider before climbing inside. It was the bathroom and toilet and as they're regularly used I hitched myself on to the landing quick.

There was no light on up here. Somewhere below I heard a radio or television, both good friends of a creeper. I was two flights up. The carpeting on the stairs was a rich pile which helped me get down faster. On the first floor a strip of light shone from under one door. I crept past and started down the last flight of stairs.

The hall lights were on. A nice silver card tray worth nicking stood on a Regency table but I brought my mind back to the job in hand. The front door was glass-panelled and as I stepped towards it a shadow appeared on the other side. I froze as the key was slipped into the lock. There was nowhere to hide in the time. The door swung open so I stepped forward to pull it back.

A girl stared up at me, the key still held in her hand at shoulder level. She was pretty and startled and wearing something vaguely green. I acted as a visitor rather than an intruder. Still holding the door for her, I smiled and stepped back so that she could pass me. She murmured 'Thank you', was just about to ask who I was when I stepped into the porch, 'Goodnight,' I said and closed the door behind me.

I turned right into the street, away from the mews and Reisen's men who were waiting for me. As I turned, I noticed the protruding bonnet of the car in the mews entrance. I grabbed the first vacant cab and asked for Shaftesbury Avenue. When I relaxed on the leather I wearily reflected that it was happening again – I was on the run, but differently from last time. Give me the fuzz any day. Odd pointers about Penny came back to me; the way she had looked at the fur shop, the car, the expensive restaurants she had insisted on, odd traces of envy in her observations. Yet these had been transitory for there were other things about her that were infinitely more noticeable, more desirable. She had disguised her greed with the practice of years. My ego was battered. I should have known better, but finding myself conned was no new experience. And I was sad because I liked her. One day she would cross the wrong man and would become another dead body on a heath. But it looked as though I would beat her to it.

I walked up to Reisen's club from Shaftesbury Avenue. I know it was a desperate act but it couldn't make things worse.

When I presented myself to the doorman he could hardly believe his eyes. Reisen's victims did not make a present of themselves. 'Tell him I want to see him,' I said. And I didn't have to wait long. When I reached the first floor for the routine search the boys eyed me curiously; they weren't used to dead men offering themselves for the coffin. 'I've come to be measured,' I said, just to put them right, and they regarded me with a new respect. What difference did it make?

Reisen kept me waiting a long time in the room where I had first met Penny. A lot of water had passed under the bridge since then. I flipped through magazines then gandered at the stock exchange prices again : the FT index was down. I waited so long that I finally went straight into Reisen's office without knocking.

There were three of them round his desk; the boss man himself in a slightly luminous gunmetal blue jacket with a good deal of white cuff showing and the inevitable cigar, Knocker Roberts, trying to push his muscles back inside a normally cut lounge suit, and another mean-looking character I didn't recognize. I invariably get light-headed when in danger; it's a sort of mental throwing-in of the towel, nothing matters any more.

They all turned to stare at me blankly and I could see that my visit had really shaken them. All I got was a deadly silence beamed by six coral-hard eyes. It gave me a brief feeling of victory.

I pointed a finger at them. 'Bang, bang, bang. You're all dead.'

It stirred them into sluggish movement; they still didn't know what to make of it. Knocker detached himself and began to approach slowly. As I couldn't expect his friendship at this stage I said to Reisen, 'If I'm not out of here soon the bloke I left outside is very definitely going to Old Bill to tell him where I am. He has strict instructions.'

It stopped Knocker in his tracks. He looked back at Reisen who shrugged, accepted the situation and told the other two to leave me to him. Knocker and the other character went reluctantly out of a side door, looking back at Reisen who was now playing it cool to show them that he could handle me on his own. Reisen remained on his feet as if expecting trouble. He took courage from a long drag at the cigar then said through a smoke cloud, 'You've got a nerve coming here. You're a dead man, d'yer know that?'

'Well, then, I've made it easier for you. All you have to do is squeeze the trigger. Would you like me to turn my back?'

'Don't be funny with me, Spider. The game's over. What d'you want?'

I approached the desk and his fingers crept up to the buzzer. Then I sat down as if I had the whole thing under control but the truth was the confrontation had made my legs weak, and I had to get the weight off them.

'You've confirmed what I've heard,' I said reasonably. 'You're out to top me, but why? What have I done to you?'

'Don't give me that clap.' Reisen sat down to show that he wasn't afraid. 'You grassed, baby. You lost me the biggest single snatch of my life and for that you die. Slowly. How d'yer like that?'

'Marvellous. We're all dying slowly anyway. You should know better than that, Rex, boy. Spider doesn't grass.'

'He did this time.'

'What makes you say that?'

'Come off it. Knocker saw you in his mirror.'

'You mean he thought he did.'

'We're wasting time. He saw you all right.'

'And then, presumably, drove straight on to dump the stuff without evasive action?'

Reisen hesitated. He had himself well under control and had got used to the idea of my being there. Besides, help was a fingertip away. 'All right. If it'll make you feel better I'll tell you. I prefer a bloke to know what he's being topped for; it makes him wish he hadn't done it all the way to the grave. Knocker *thought* he saw you. But you were clever and he didn't see you again. He thought nothing more of it until the fuzz surrounded the place and we'd lost over two million quid on the open market. Then we went into it more deeply. The bent lead on the window downstairs; neat but you couldn't get it back as it had been. Then the dog. We found out about that. It was a very good job, Spider, I'll give you that. Your type of job. But not good enough. Then Knocker thought more carefully about whether he had spotted you.' He opened his arms expansively, the smoke forming a couple of rings.

'Wouldn't stand up in court,' I challenged. 'Very circumstantial.'

'It stood up in ours, boy. A jury of two passed a verdict in three minutes.'

'So if I say this is all a lot of cobblers you won't believe me.'

'That's right.'

'And if you afterwards find out that you've topped the wrong bloke that won't worry you either?'

'Right again, except that the extra topping will cost me more.'

'Tell me, why should I grass on a job that I was on myself and stood to make over twenty grand?'

'Drugs. I told you before that you had scruples that don't belong in a villain.'

'Then as I'm for the chop anyway, tell me why you dragged me into it in the first place?'

'Dragged you in? I applied a little pressure to get you to do the job.'

'That's not what I'm talking about. Alan Bruce Chapman. You were in it up to your neck. You tried to use me as a red herring. Why?'

'You've gone round the bend, boy. Still, you haven't got to suffer much longer.'

'Listen, Rexy. You said yourself that I have friends in high places. You'd better bear it in mind. You own the house where Chapman holed up. And it's obvious that you sprung him. The great patriot Reisen. There are certain people who might think that you shot him as well. If they don't think it now they will when I've finished with them.' It was all I had to offer. My last fling, but I realized that it could easily swing it more the other way.

As I watched I saw that I was halfway to success. His expression blanked up and he focused on middle distance; the cigar did its chimney-stack act and for a while he was completely still, taking his time, figuring it out. When a trace of confusion flickered in his eyes I knew I had lost. If in doubt snuff 'em out. It had always worked for him. He wasn't going to change tactics now. He stirred to life and I wished he hadn't. His gaze shot an extra few feet to meet mine and I experienced the chilliest feeling of my life. This was the scared Reisen taking the only effective remedy he knew.

He was in no doubt now and his continued silence made it worse. I felt like the earth was being shovelled on top of me while I was still breathing. He spoke at last and I wasn't expecting reassurance.

'You made a mistake coming 'ere, Spider. You're a good creeper but a bloody fool. I was going to let it drag out a bit, make you sweat before your concrete boots hit the drink. Now I'll have to do it straightaway. You shouldn't threaten me, boy. No one's ever done that and got away with it. That's why I'm top of the heap.'

I rose, annoyed that I had to use one hand as leverage. But I was feeling worse now than when I came in.

Reisen pressed the buzzer like he was signalling in morse. The side door opened and Knocker and the other mean character came in. Behind me I heard the other door open. I considered rushing Reisen but he opened his drawer and pulled out a thick long-bladed knife not far short of the old-fashioned bayonet. It had been rumoured that this was his favourite weapon and now I was seeing for myself. It had some strange psychological effect on him for his expression glazed over and his hand began to tremble. The fact that he seemed scared to use it wasn't going to help me. In the process of proving to himself that he could use it he could shred me to bloody ribbons. He got a grip on himself in front of the others and said for effect, 'Sit down, Spider. You're not going anywhere without your boots on.'

CHAPTER 13

He meant concrete boots, of course. I stood where I was and looked at my watch. 'Just over five minutes,' I warned. 'That's all you've got to let me out of here before my mate goes to the fuzz.'

'Balls,' Reisen said equably. 'Don't give me that. Sit down.'

'Please youself,' I said, sitting; it was better than being knocked down. 'You're getting careless, Rexy. Doing it on your own doorstep. Your strength has always been no visible link between you and your victim. Yet here I am in your very own office with someone waiting outside while you top me here.'

It had its effect. Reisen suddenly realized that he couldn't afford to get careless at this stage. He nodded to Knocker. 'Nip down and see if you can find anyone outside.'

I smiled but it cost me a lot. 'He's wearing a yellow suit with a blue carnation and a copy of yesterday's *Times* under his left arm at an angle of forty-five degrees,' I said to Knocker. Then to Reisen. 'Just how stupid do you think I am? I knew the finger was on me when I arrived. Do you think I'd just barge straight in here without help? What do you think I've done, posted a uniformed sentry outside? You won't see my man.'

Reisen said nothing to me but gave a nodded instruction to Knocker which sent him on his way. That still left someone behind me and the mean-looking character by the side door in addition to Reisen himself. It was too many. My best chance was still bluff but I didn't rate it too much. To fill in time and take my mind off Knocker's return I said, 'I can't understand why you wanted me for the airport job anyway. Any driver would have done.' But Reisen wasn't being drawn. Whatever his reasons for using me, they no longer mattered to him. 'I wonder how many people saw me come in here,' I remarked conversationally. I think Reisen wondered too, for I saw a flicker of annoyance cross his face. He was on home ground and was beginning to regret it. His agitation showed when the mean character suggested that he cut me up a bit to keep me quiet and Reisen nearly bit his head off.

Knocker came bursting back into the room and my spirits fell although they had little distance to travel. 'There's no one I can pinpoint, Rex. People milling about in the usual way but no one who looks like a stake out.'

Reisen looked over to me not knowing what to believe. I looked at my watch again and shrugged. 'Wherever he might have been when Knocker went down I can assure you that he's not here now. He's on his way to the fuzz.'

The phone rang and we all jumped. Reisen grabbed it, then concentrated on me while he answered in a series of low monosyllables. Finally he said, 'He's here now. You OK?'

I guessed that Penny had freed herself and was making her report.

Reisen put down the phone, gave me a stare of subdued hatred and said, 'Get out of here.'

I didn't want to seem too eager so I rose quite slowly hoping that he wouldn't notice the real reason. 'What changed your mind?'

'Get out fast,' he snapped again.

But I could guess the reason. Penny may have told him that I was likely to have taken precautions. So he wasn't willing to take the risk. He wouldn't want the fuzz here.

When I was halfway across the room he instructed Knocker. 'I want him tailed wherever he goes. I want him under our eye one way or the other for twenty-four hours a day, starting from now. And when he's holed himself up nice and lonely like, I want him as carved up as you like as long as he's still alive. Don't overdo it but have some fun. D'yer get that, Spider. How d'yer like that?'

I turned to face him and said, 'Don't forget to let the bookings still go through the XYY Agency. If I disappear at the time the bookings stop it will look bad for you, won't it? Even a *bent* copper could figure that one.'

He nearly had a stroke because he knew I was right; he couldn't change anything businesswise yet and the realization almost choked him. If you're going to make an enemy make a good one.

Now that it was time to leave I was reluctant to go. I was safe here. My real problems would begin once I was outside. A sideways glance to Knocker produced no change. Friendship only flowered while things were right. It would be useless to turn to him for help, even compassion. Knocker would happily top me if told to and enjoy the bonus at the end of it.

The mobster at the main office door stood aside for me as I reached it. Reisen, realizing my feelings, jeered, 'What's wrong, boy? Nowhere to go?'

The others laughed. As I walked through the doorway I was aware of a very hollow victory. So I took my time down the stairs aware that Reisen's boys were following my back with a professional sort of interest, perhaps wondering how I would take it when the moment came. And they weren't alone in that.

I had to take the step that finally landed me in the street and I stood outside the door which remained open as at least two other people followed me out. Provided I stayed put I was still reasonably safe, or as long as I kept to crowded places. But even Soho emptied some time. The worst thing I could do would be to panic so I stood there planning my next move.

The streets were busy, the restaurant and theatre crowds milling about, and the strip clubs taking a quick turnover. The boys behind me were in no hurry. They could stick as close as they liked; it was all good unnerving stuff. Just now they simply grouped in the doorway behind me, literally breathing down my neck. There was no refinement with these boys.

The truth was I had nowhere to go. Even if I shook off this bunch what happened next? I couldn't go home, nor to Maggie's empty flat. If I holed up in an hotel word would filter back. There was no ultimate escape. So I was snookered. It was a very lonely feeling.

Someone behind nudged me forward but I carry enough weight to stand my ground. I turned and snarled, 'What do you want to do, start something on his doorstep?' Which kept them off me, but I'd have to make a move soon.

I walked slowly down to Shaftesbury Avenue knowing that I was safe because we were too near Reisen's and there were too many people about. Three of the boys came with me, almost as if we were all walking together. Suddenly I sprinted forward and they thundered after me. I stopped as soon as I was round the corner and they came clumping by, pulling up as they went past me. It had been a try on. Two I could outrun, I was certain of that, but the third, a short, slight fellow with a razor gash near his eye was quick on his feet so he was the one I had to watch.

Continuing towards Piccadilly I suddenly jumped on to a passing bus going in the opposite direction. It had just crossed a set of lights and was picking up speed as I landed on its platform. I knew that the small fellow would be just behind me so I swung my body across the rear of the platform, keeping my hand firmly on the rail. As he leaped forward to grab the rail my swinging body knocked him back. He made a lunge at my jacket but I was well balanced enough to back-heel him on his shin as his toe sought purchase on the fraction of platform I had left him. He fell off and when I looked back was flat on his face with a taxi hovering over him. A pedestrian shook his fist at me as he eceded down Shaftesbury Avenue. So there was now another little matter for Reisen's boys to sort out with me when they finally caught up. And they would. As the conductor was upstairs I dropped off just before the next stop and headed towards Piccadilly along the back doubles around Lisle Street. I hailed a cab and headed for Penny's place.

I paid him off just before we reached the mews, nosed about to make sure the lads had all been called off, walked quietly down the mews, and silently let myself into the cottage. I scouted around the ground floor without finding her. She had eaten something; plates were drying on the draining board. I went upstairs. The smell of perfume and steam reached me and then I heard the splash of water. I stepped into the bathroom without knocking.

She almost died of fright but I couldn't get worked up about it. Full length in the bath, her hair tied at the nape of the neck with red ribbon, she started a scream that packed up on her and her hands flew up to cover her breasts. Very white, she sat staring at me in stark terror. Hooking the cork-topped bath stool forward I sat on it and eyed her quietly. 'Suits you,' I said. 'You've got good skin but when it's white like that it looks as translucent as very fine china.' It was my day for giving her shocks so I threw in the compliment.

She recovered a little but her breathing was hard, water trickling over her round shoulders and between her breasts. She wanted to wipe water from her eyes but kept her hands cupped until finally she unsuccessfully tried it with a wet arm.

Picking up a towel I held it by each end, then snapped it taut. 'Here, let me do it,' I approached slowly.

Cringing back in the bath she said, 'You come near me and I'll scream my head off.'

'You scream your head off and I'll disconnect the wire from the heating coil and ram the live ends in the water. I'm on a loser whatever I do, Penny. Thirty years for topping you might be better than what Reisen has in store for me.'

She was frightened all right, but she came back. 'He'd get you in the nick, as you well know. He'd make it a living death for you. And when you came out after ten or twelve he'd still finish you off.'

I handed her the towel but she wouldn't lower her hands. 'For God's sake,' I exclaimed, 'it's a bit late for that sort of modesty between us, isn't it? I'm not here to rape you.'

She lowered her hands and briefly I wished the clock could be put back. She dried her face and then took the big bath towel I handed her. She stood up, using the towel ineffectively to cover herself. Even now I found her desirable and as one long leg came groping for the bathmat I had to hold myself back.

The mat darkened where she stood. Leaning over, she pulled out the plug and swished the water around. Well, I had plenty of time, too. She didn't intend to dry in front of me so she stood there with the towel draped round her.

'Would you like the stool?' I offered without rising.

'Why have you come back?'

'Not to harm you. Look, I find it disconcerting seeing you standing like that. Let's face it: twenty-four hours ago we were still ardent lovers. I'll wait for you outside while you get dressed.'

'It won't help you. It would be better if you went.' By now she had regained composure but was still uncertain of me. Droplets ran over her lips and down her chin and I could see faint marks where the adhesive tape had been.

'You're still very lovely,' I said. 'It's a pity you are what you are. I'll wait.'

'You're wasting your time,' she snapped as I left her to it.

She didn't hurry, hoping perhaps that I would go. Then she went to the bedroom and I heard her shoot the door-bolt so I called out, 'If you don't take that bolt off I'll smash down the door.' The bolt clicked back again. I started whistling to remind her that I was still there.

When she finally came out her feet were bare and she wore a plain black skirt and lemon blouse. The ribbon was still in her hair. From her point of view I was probably seeing her at her worst; she wore no make-up and was slightly flushed from the steam of the bath. But to me she looked young and fresh and was marred only by a rigidity of expression. I wondered if the hardness went all through.

'You look great,' I said. It was a sincere compliment but it roused nothing in her. She gave me a cool upward glance from under her dark lashes but I could have been a stranger. Again I got a hollow feeling.

'I want to talk to you,' I suggested.

'There's nothing to discuss. After what you called me and did to me you've got a nerve coming here.' She was speaking in a monotone, all expression gone. I didn't answer; there was no winning with that sort of mood. We went into the lounge and the atmosphere was charged with gloom. She was tolerating the situation because there was little she could do and she wanted to keep the temperature down. It was almost impossible to imagine the enveloping passion of her straining in my arms such a little time ago. I had to try to bring her back to that point.

'You probably know that I called on Rex. I believe you phoned while I was there.'

She gazed across noncommittally, swinging one leg slowly over the other.

'He laid it on the line for me,' I explained. 'They'll cut me, then top me.'

No answer. She was studying her toes. I was going to get no help from her.

'They'll put my feet into a tray of wet concrete, wait for it to set, leave me like that for a while, not to give me time to pray but hoping I'll see the error of my ways and crack into a gibbering, pleading animal.'

There was no response but she had clasped her hands together and was straining at them. She made no attempt to look at me.

'When they're ready they'll cart me off to some quiet spot in the dead of night and sit me on the parapet. They'll joke and sneer and deride me and finally push, and there I am in the water, still alive with my hands free but with no power to save myself. Like an idiot I'll hold my breath for a long as I can in the hope that some concrete-eating piranha lurks below. My arms will flail about in an impossible attempt to bring me to the surface. The bloke you've been sleeping with the past weeks will be rotting vegetation on the river bed.'

She was very pale now, her fingers intertwined, knuckles white. At last she looked up at me and in a very quiet unsteady voice she said, 'And if I try to help you in any way I'll finish up like you, but I won't be so strong and they'll have all the gibbering they want.'

I had aroused in her a spark of pity but she was still looking after number one. It was a start.

'You don't know what I have in mind. There's no risk for you.'

'There must be.'

'Do you know what they're topping me for?'

'No. I don't want to know.'

My heart sank at that. It meant that she had set me up without even asking why. She had obeyed instructions; period. If she was *that* hard I was wasting my time.

'Reisen thinks I followed Knocker. All you have to do is to say I was with you. He'll believe you.'

'*Did* you follow him?'

'You must be mad; of course I didn't, but someone grassed and Reisen thinks it's me.'

'And you honestly expect me to tell Reisen that?'

'Why not? You've done everything he's asked of you; spied on me, set me up. Why should he be suspicious? Ask him why he's doing it and when he tells you explain that I was with you from half-six, then he'll know that I couldn't have been following Knocker.'

'I'm sorry for you, Willie, but I can't do it. I'm too scared for myself.'

'Look, you're a lovely girl. You've got to live with yourself. One day you're going to suffer terrible remorse for all this. Here's a chance to set it right, to wipe out what you've already done to me.'

She looked away in agitation but I think it was from my pressure and not indecision on her part. 'No. There will be no remorse, I can promise you.' Then she looked up quickly and threw it all back at me. 'If you can give me a guarantee that Reisen will take a sane view of it, I'll do it.'

She had played against my basic honesty; a villain I may be but there are some things I won't do at any price. With my record why I should be lumbered with a conscience I've never understood. I couldn't reply. Not to that. So I struck out at her own weakness. I was lowering myself but it was all a matter of values. I enjoyed life and I valued it more than money. To Penny the two were synonymous.

'I'll give you a partnership in my business. That I *can* guarantee. Shared profits.' Fighting for my life and it had come to this, for she was the only one who could help me.

And she considered it. I had struck at her core and as I sat watching her mull it over I was sickened more than by her original betrayal. I shouldn't have been surprised because I had broached it myself but there was something unhealthily calculated in her pose. She was giving far more thought to the proposition than to the fact that I was for the chop. Her hands had stopped twitching as she worked it out behind hard eyes.

Through rising nausea I heard myself say, 'Forget it. I find the price too high to pay.' I would never live with it after and I've always found contempt of myself unbearable. I lacked her ability to shut out my weaknesses.

She looked coolly across. 'It makes no difference; I wasn't going to accept anyway. I doubt your profit margins are worth the risk.'

Wearily I stretched. I looked at her and didn't know her; two strangers unattracted to each other.

'There's one more thing,' I said, 'which will cost you nothing. Do you know why Reisen has taken all this trouble to involve me?'

She had now lost all interest if ever there had been any. 'No. And if I did I wouldn't tell you. It might incriminate me.'

I went into the hall. She stood in front of me, arms

crossed, and she gazed at me in a detached way that I found disturbing. What a waste of beauty. There was nothing more between us. We didn't say another word. I nodded briefly and let myself out. As I stepped into the mews I was feeling more sorry for her than for myself but by the time I reached the corner the feeling was reversed.

What now? I simply didn't know. I had enough money with me for a few nights' accommodation. But a man without luggage is like a man in a white suit. Reisen would want to get hold of me as soon as he could just in case there was something in my threat.

In despair I took myself down to the Embankment to watch the slow-moving Thames make a jigsaw puzzle of the lights flooding from the Festival Hall on the far bank. A barge came pushing by, dark and silent, carving a great moving chunk out of the puzzle. I felt emptier than I can remember. I bought a cup of tea and a hot dog at the coffee stall near the railway arches. But these places were vulnerable; a Reisen car could tour the stalls. So I moved on and sat on one of the slatted Embankment seats. This too was dangerous. I sat and watched people, traffic and the back of the Savoy Hotel as the plane trees darkened into silhouettes. It was warm and the sky was turning purple. I should have been sitting here enjoying it instead of dreading the next move.

In the distance I saw a car pull up at the coffee stall and a man stepped out; even from here I knew that it was no copper. I got up and moved towards Blackfriars Bridge. It wasn't difficult for Reisen. The places I could go to were strictly limited. Just as I knew where to look for a hidden key, he knew the main points I might follow.

The car came along at a fair speed, went past on the opposite side of the road and continued in the thinning stream. I had seen this out of the corner of my eye as I kept my head half-averted. It may have had nothing to do with Reisen, but every little incident like that would smack of danger.

I crossed the wide stretch of Embankment beside the small gardens. There were few people about. The office blocks had closed hours ago and this was not theatre or restaurant land. Although in the heart of London the Embankment can be a lonely place at night.

It was the car's tail-lights that warned me. From this distance it could have been any car but I could only hope to survive by being suspicious of everything. This particular car had turned left farther up but its nearside tail-light just protruded beyond the building line. It might have been there for a long time but its line of focus pulled my sight to furtive figures hugging shadows as they came towards me. I looked round. A man following a little distance behind me checked momentarily. He hadn't expected me to turn.

The car had dropped one man off as a tail and the others were now coming back. The alternative routes were limited : the river on my right and the gardens on my left. The bloke behind had twigged that I was alerted so he started to close the gap. I didn't wait. I ran into the gardens over a carefully nurtured flowerbed and began to pick my way through.

A road circled the gardens but Reisen's boys would know it too. Feet scraped behind me. These blokes weren't creepers; they were having difficulty keeping the noise down. It gave me another few seconds and, bent low, I covered a lot of ground heading east.

To my left the bandstand stuck out like a spectred canopy. The fragrance of spring flowers came off the rich soil. The gardens were too accessible from the road. There were no railings and several entrances. Running footsteps sounded ahead of me. Someone blundered into the shrub and swore as his foot caught a root. There were at least three of them but this was my game not theirs.

Sound of them faded as they fanned out. Keeping quite still I plotted their movements. There was no cohesion and I knew they'd be happier back on the streets where there were intersections to cut off. They couldn't use torches; it would attract the fuzz. Listening carefully, I moved slowly as I located their advance.

I slipped up to the densest part of the garden on the Savoy Hotel side, buried myself in the thick foliage and wondered what best to do. If I got back on to the pavement and ran they'd hear me and they had a car.

Someone used a torch. I was well bedded down but not far enough to avoid a beam. Then the other two got brave and suddenly there were three beams probing the flowerbeds, two angled from the front and one from behind. Nor were they caring about noise any more; they simply blundered along like beaters in a hunt.

Now that they were being positive they coordinated better. When they heard the footsteps of a passing couple they switched off until they had passed and listened in case I moved. I did move, but slowly, up towards the back of the garden where it met a low wall which dipped on to the narrow curved street at the back of the Savoy. I could see the hotel lights through the glass doors.

The torches flashed again much closer and moving much faster. It was a clumsy search but it was urgent and thorough.

The torch beams swept over the flowerbeds very quickly. It was on the Savoy side that the real probing went on and now they were running, darting their beams into the thick green foliage and getting the knack of the shadows they created.

Lying flat on the damp earth I rolled back until I was overhanging the street. Gently I lowered myself on to the pavement. I didn't dare stand up because I'd be visible above the low wall and between the gaps of plants. So I crawled along on hands and knees and, to my dismay, saw a uniformed doorman just inside the Savoy back entrance. At the moment he couldn't see me but when I passed the strip of light thrown out from the hotel interior he must.

If I rose I would be seen from the gardens and if I continued crawling along the doorman would ring for the fuzz fast. Reaching the danger zone of light I knew I couldn't wait for ever because Reisen's boys would fan round the perimeter streets.

The doorman turned his back and I was just about to take a chance when a taxi came round the bend towards me. I just flattened myself with the hopelessness of it. It would bring Reisen's boys running in case I dived for it. Suddenly everything was going wrong.

CHAPTER 14

The taxi slowed and pulled up outside the hotel back entrance. The ever-alert doorman had the door open and two Americans climbed out, audibly discussing the merits of the Prospect of Whitby, the old smuggling pub farther up the Thames. They drew the doorman into it and while the cabby was collecting his fare I scrambled past like an injured crab.

The new danger was that Reisen's boys would come running from the gardens to see what the cab was up to. I took a calculated risk. Reckoning that by now I must have passed the spot where the front torchman had reached I climbed back into the gardens and moved among the plants like an alley cat. Even as I moved I heard one of Reisen's men step out of the gardens and sensed that he was watching the cab. When it pulled away without a fare I heard him ask the doorman if he had seen a Scots terrier which had run into the gardens and which he and his friends were searching for. It was a crafty move which allayed the doorman.

But I kept going towards the point where the road curved round to meet the Embankment. The nearer I got the more cagey I became. Because the thick growth diminished I finished up doing an elbow crawl flat on my belly. Peering through some rhododendrons I spotted the car still parked just by a side road. They hadn't been so stupid as to leave it unattended; the driver was pacing up and down, peering into the gardens, and beating his fists together.

It was difficult. I couldn't just step out. Behind me the torches were at it again, working their way outward from a central point where the men must all have met up.

Looking at matey through the leaves didn't reassure me; he appeared a right thug, with baggy trousers and an anorak zipped up to the neck. As two of the others were heading back my way I had to make a decision.

I crept as near to the edge as I dare. The bloke near the car couldn't have been more than a dozen feet from me but he was peering over me towards the moving lights. His restlessness carried him up and down on a short beat as if he was caged, his hands for ever moving threateningly. Bringing my feet up under me I prepared to spring. He came thumping along again and almost put me off. When he was within six feet I sprang.

For a thick-set bloke he moved easily, surprised, but pivoting neatly on his feet as I lunged out at him. He partially blocked my blows as his arms came up in a boxer's stance. I didn't like the neat movement of his feet, either. I hurt him but he rode some of it and instead of falling flat he came back at me with a nasty, knowing grin on his ugly face. I had one advantage; it was my life they were after.

I waded in with such a flurry of blows that he had to cover up to protect his head. But he was well under control, riding, weaving, covering, using his feet like a pro. I upped my output, knowing that it couldn't last and wondered when he would remember to yell for the others.

I wasn't getting through enough to do him real damage. Finally I forced him back on one leg and kicked the other sticking out straight on the shin. That brought his guard down as he yelled in agony. He roared a blasphemy at me while I thumped his open jaw and this time he staggered back. But he was tough as a stonecast cottage. He wouldn't go down. In agony with his leg he came limping at me with reddened eyes and fists moving for a kill. Leaning back I almost overbalanced and just when he thought he had me I stuck my long leg out again to run it down his already damaged shin. He screamed and I thumped him again. God! he was made of rock. Half-out, he clinched instinctively, head against my chest while I tried to shake him off. I could hear the others running fast towards us.

While matey was holding on like grim death he tried a few vicious heel-tapping manoeuvres that had me jumping. I was getting desperate às the footsteps pounded nearer. Upping my muscle power I pushed matey as hard as I could and backed off quickly. In his dazed state he knew only one direction and came straight back at me, his arms out like a blinded wrestler. There was no time left. I couldn't manage this one, never mind another three. I flung a bolo over his arm and clumped him solidly on the side of his head. His knees began to go but I didn't wait.

I reached the car as the others reached the garden bank. Jumping in, the first thing I did was to lock all the doors from the inside. I managed the last one as the unholy trio burst around me, tugging at doors and crashing at the car roof and windows. It was a terrible sensation seeing their snarling faces. Almost too scared to look for the ignition key in case it wasn't there I felt a sweeping relief when I saw the key tab hanging down. The car started at once.

The engine noise drove the three mobsters berserk. One started tearing at the bonnet, trying to lever it up so that he could cut the engine from underneath, while the other two hammered away at the doors. Then one stooped and I realized with panic that he was going to knife the tyre. If they had all had the same idea I'd have had it. Ramming her in gear made the bonnet man throw himself in front of the car like a civil disobedience demonstrator. I reversed in a flash and the car lurched back with two of the boys holding doors, one of whom was smashing at my window with the butt of a pistol. The car movement took the steam out of his blow. I couldn't hurtle into the Embankment for fear of hitting another car so I braked sharply which half-threw them, rapidly changed gear and hurtled forward straight for the third thug who was still prone in front of me. He moved faster than at any time in his life, sensing that I was willing to go straight over him.

The crack of the nearside bumper catching his legs made me feel sick. I caught a glimpse of him rolling away contorted in agony, and of the one I had socked still on his knees swaying and holding his bowed face in his hands. I felt the others let go as I accelerated and then I was skidding round the bend of the road.

The Savoy doorman stepped out as I roared past and it felt as if the tension of years had built up to breaking point in me and only speed could release it. I had left behind a nightmare but was perhaps driving straight into another one. I took corners without conscious thought of direction and once ignored a red light. The wheel turned in my hands and it was a good half-hour later before I realized that I was heading fast down the A40 on the Oxford road.

Calmer, I moved her into the slow lane and kept her there. There was no hurry any more. I had nowhere to go. Reisen wasn't going to report the car stolen, for the last thing he wanted was me in the hands of the fuzz. Yet for how long could I keep this up? When they got their hands on me I'd be lucky to make the river.

The car had plenty of juice so I kept her rolling aimlessly. Then I suddenly thought of a safe billet for the night and pulled out into the middle lane.

I dumped the car in a car park behind some flats over shops in Amersham-on-the-Hill. She would probably remain there for days before anyone became curious and meanwhile I could help myself if I needed her. This, too, was an area where Reisen would have to scratch hard to find the right contacts. It was about ten minutes' walk from the car park to the old house where the opium had been hidden in the deep-freeze.

Standing on the fringe of the gravel drive it was clear that the house was deserted. There were no lights, no sign of life at all. Certainly the police weren't watching it from this side, although they could easily hide in the spare plot. Taking the circular route I landed at the back of the house, then up the garden to the window I had broken through. Tiredness and desperation were making me careless. All I knew as I gazed at the blank leaded windows was that I just didn't have the energy to break in the hard way. It was too quiet but as I rammed my elbow into the glass most of it fell in on to the fitted carpet. I had the sense to wait to see if the neighbours had heard, then unlocked the window and climbed in.

It had the smell of emptiness. The curtains were drawn back so that it was too risky to use my pencil torch. I went upstairs, treading quietly from habit, but not caring about the odd groans from old wood. It was a sign of weariness and of increasing resignation to my fate.

In the bedroom where the couple had quarrelled I risked my torch as the room faced the screen of beeches. The bed was unmade so I pulled up the blankets and put a pillow on top. Something squeaked loudly as I trod on it and as I jumped back I realized that it was a rubber top for the dog. Poor old Jik; I supposed someone was looking after him while his owners sweated in nick. I stretched out on the bed fully clothed, shoes still on, while weariness swept over me in such gusts that I fell asleep with Jik's toy still in my hand.

The sun woke me, hitting me straight in the eyes. Through the small leaded panes it rode low like a flaming traffic beacon, barely topping the trees and sending shafts through the leaves. The birds were belting away and when I risked a look out they were lining up along the terrace waiting for the regular meal which today would not come.

It was unlikely that Reisen would send anyone down here so soon after the police raid and I felt reasonably safe. I had a bath but couldn't empty it for the outlet pipe ran down the front of the house and the gurgle might be heard. I shaved too, borrowing some gear I found. Then I raided the deep-freeze and took out a couple of steaks, potato croquettes and some *petit pois*, putting them out to thaw in the kitchen. I made some coffee and boiled a couple of eggs to eat with toast and marmalade. There was enough food laid in for a seige.

It would be foolish to leave the house in daylight so I made myself comfortable and considered how to solve the insoluble. The only way to get Reisen off my back was to top him or pin something on him. I'd never get near enough to top him, even if I was the type. But I must strike back.

So what could I find to blackmail him with; what information was worth my life?

He was the sort of bloke to keep two sets of books and somewhere he had to keep a pay register. There might be evidence of big jobs floating in some safe place like spare tom too hot to be pushed out for a while. If there were such things they would be well hidden; they'd hardly be in the safe in his office. I didn't figure Reisen as a safe-deposit man, he'd have his own deposit box and I didn't think it would be far from him.

All this was very vague but it was all I had. I might dig out snide associations which had to be accounted for, like the house where Chapman had holed up. That was the only one that I knew about. If I could produce a few shady snippets to be opened only in the event of my death it *could* haul him off.

This boiled down to one very simple fact. The only way to get anything against Reisen was to break into his offices. The thought didn't scare me as much as it should have because I'm a creeper and that's my sort of game. But I wasn't kidding myself, either. Reisen wouldn't leave stuff around without it being well hidden and carefully protected. His safety depended on it as much as mine depended on winkling it out, and his resources were far superior. And yet in the very remote chance of success I might come up with the answer to Reisen involving me.

I rang my office from the phone in the downstairs study. Young Charlie Hewitt answered and if he had half an idea of the scrape I was in he'd have given in his notice then. We chatted about the business, then I asked him if Smoky Joe was there. He was.

'Smoky,' I said, 'listen carefully. I want some polo ajax, a couple of detonators and a drill. Now can you lay your hands on some? Get the money from Charlie Hewitt.' I could almost see his eyes going round.

'Listen, boss.' His voice went quiet and I guessed that he was afraid of the others hearing. 'You can hole up in ma lace. There's just abaht room. Nem mind this explosive tuff. Don't you go doing nothing silly.'

'Smoky, I haven't the time to argue. Thanks for your offer. I won't forget it but I won't do it. Now I want the plastic, detonators, wire and plasticine, but it's the bang tuff that's difficult. Try Johnnie Jackson or, failing him, Inky Penn. And for God's sake don't say it's for me. Now will you try?'

'Ah'll try but ah don' like it.'

'I'm relying on you, Smoky.' I gave him the telephone number to ring me and then asked him to hand me back to Charlie Hewitt. 'Charlie,' I said to show him what a democratic boss I was, 'cash a cheque for two hundred pounds and give the money to Smoky. He's collecting something for me.'

'But I can only sign a cheque for fifty.' Trust Charlie to get his facts right.

'Then make out four bloody cheques for fifty,' I roared, forgetting to be friendly. 'And Charlie, it must be done now. I'm relying on you.'

I didn't expect to succeed, but just doing something made me feel better. I would have liked to go up to Soho and do some casing in daylight but it was out of the question.

I took stock of what I had on me in the way of breaking-and-entering gear. I always carry a pencil torch, crocodile clip, a penknife, a few keys, my little spatula gadget, a glass cutter, mica and a nail file. It wasn't much for a job like this. I don't know how he rated for alarms but I certainly hadn't noticed any in his office. His main protection was his reputation; only a maniac would screw him and I wasn't arguing with my own appraisal.

Searching the house for extra equipment produced nothing but a bent screwdriver. The tools would be in the garage and I couldn't go out to it in case I was seen.

The food was good. The kitchen smelled after my cooking because I couldn't use the Vent Axia. Time was dragging like a ball and chain. I had far too much time to think.

The phone rang while I was squatting in the lounge reading an old magazine. I jumped out of my seat as the bell went like a fire alarm in the empty house. Diving for the study I whipped the receiver off its cradle while peering through the windows to see if anyone was about.

'Yes?' I was ready to tell someone it was the wrong number.

'That you, boss?' Smoky was being cautious too.

'Smoky?'

'Ah got the jelly. Had to pay high.'

'Never mind the cost. Did you get it all?'

'All you ordered. It's in your office.'

'Christ! Don't let the staff see it. Now look, I want to pick it up tonight somewhere safe. Not the office. Reisen will keep an eye on the office.'

'What d'you plan to do, boss?'

'It won't help you to know, Smoky. Do you think Reisen's watching you?'

'Ah dunno. Maybe we'd better think the worst.'

'Right. You'll find a couple of airline cabin bags in my office; put the stuff in one of those and take it home. It's safe as long as you keep the detonators separate from the explosive and don't put them near heat. Keep the kids away from it. Now is there anyone you can trust to deliver the stuff to me at Trafalgar Square? It can't be you in case you're watched.'

'Ah can find someone.'

'Be real careful, Smoky. It mustn't be anyone remotely connected with Reisen. Whoever it is, send them to the men's toilet in Trafalgar Square Tube Station. Tell him to go into any cubicle at precisely eleven o'clock but to only half-lock the door so that I can identify the half-engaged half-vacant sign. He waits five minutes and comes out without the stuff. You got that?'

Smoky repeated it faithfully, and that was as far as I could go. Eleven o'clock was putting me on the streets far too early but I wasn't sure what time the Tube and the toilets closed. I didn't like the plan, it was too bitty, too risky trusting someone I didn't know to deliver. But it was all I could come up with. Smoky wasn't a peterman and might have been fobbed off with anything. This was no way to start any sort of job, let alone a drum like Reisen's.

Ossie Jenkins kept coming into my mind. I could see his bloated face on the slab and realized that someone soon would be looking down at me; seeing the puffy, lifeless mess and saying, 'Poor old Spider!' And in a few days I'd be forgotten by all bar Maggie. I wanted her back badly; I always did when I was in trouble and belatedly I was beginning to repent. She deserved better.

Night came all too slowly. I made myself a final pot of tea and washed the pot afterwards.

I left by the front door. The sky was quite clear, which was a pity; a little cloud would have been helpful. The car was where I'd left it and had plenty of juice.

At this time of night it was an easy run through the dark-end Chalfonts and up as far as Shepherd's Bush. There was a traffic problem at the White City with the greyhound racing crowds but after that it was reasonable, even along Oxford Street.

I dumped the car on a parking bay. In the morning it would be discovered by a traffic warden but by the time that happened I'd either be a very wet corpse or in the clear, so I wasn't too worried.

I was getting on to dangerous territory; Soho was only a ten-minute walk away and I was fifteen minutes early; all I could do with them was to walk around. It was very lonely at this time and I began to listen to the echo of my own footfalls. Back at Trafalgar Square I timed it as close as I could, then crossed the Strand to the Tube entrance. Down I went, bearing left along the Cockspur Street tunnel where the toilets are.

As soon as I saw the toilet entrances I realized what a terrible mistake I had made. They were boarded up because they were being rebuilt. I should have known but I'd had no reason to come down here for months. There was no one near them, only myself in an empty tunnel which began to whisper what a fool I was. Suddenly I felt trapped. Did I go on or go back? Decision was cut dead by the sound of soft footsteps approaching from the Cockspur Street exit.

CHAPTER 15

If you're afraid of something go out and meet it. My old man had drummed that into me and right or wrong it had stuck. I moved in the direction of the footsteps, which the echoes turned into a stocking-footed army. The tunnel curved in a wide arc before straightening towards the street steps. A young Negro lad came into sight, saw me with widening eyes because he hadn't heard me approach, then started to flee the other way.

'It's me, Spider,' I yelled and the tiled walls picked up the cry, carrying it down to the boy as if there was a voice every yard of the way. The sound hung around like a dying wind after the words had stopped. He hesitated, looked back, and it was then that I saw the carrier-bag screwed under his arm.

'You're Smoky's son, Vincent, aren't you?' He wasn't so much reassured as hypnotized as I slowly approached with fatherly cluckings. 'It's OK, Vincent. You been before?'

'The toilets are blocked up. Dad said to make sure to see you but not to hang around so I've been coming back.'

'OK. Let's have it.' I took the bag, holding it by its string handles. 'You tell your dad that I said he's to pay you well. You get back now, and thanks.'

He went off in his soft creepers as if he couldn't get away fast enough. He sensed something wrong about the whole business and I suppose didn't want his father mixed up in it. I was angry at Smoky for risking his son in this way, yet saw it too as a tremendous compliment. His son he could trust.

I dived into a phone booth, and examined the contents of the bag. The explosive, detonators and flex were there and so was a small stick of plasticine. The drill was manual and I thought, Christ, it will take me all night. Now I had to spirit myself away for a few hours.

Soho was quiet. There was the odd furtive noise because the area never really rested.

Hours later my tiredness ebbed as action became imminent. Most of the clubs had closed except for odd basement dives where drink was obtainable almost round the clock. As I nipped down the nearest side street to Reisen's place the only noise was from scavenging rats. I tested a few drainpipes and was left undecided. This was old property, most of it decaying. Some of the pipes were far from securely fixed to the walls. I always climbed a pipe with my feet against the wall either side of it. That way I sort of walk up.

The peaceful near-silence was uncanny in this district where it didn't belong. In the habit of wearing a belt because of its many uses I threaded it through the bag handle and rebuckled it.

I heard the double tread of coppers and then a shuffling halt as doors were tried and lamps flashed into cavities. It was best that I was on my way before they got too near. Taking a chance on what I reckoned the strongest pipe, I started up, hoping that it would hold all the way to the top; if it didn't Reisen wouldn't have to worry any more. The smell of rotting garbage followed me up on the warm night air. The two coppers were nearer than I had reckoned and I had to stop climbing when I heard them below me. I looked down and saw flashlamps probing into corners. They only had to swing them up to see me clinging to the pipe. Hovering like that was a tremendous strain and when they lit up cigarettes my spirits sank. I couldn't hold my position for long.

The glowing cigarettes disappeared into cupped hands and the coppers continued down Dean Street. My muscles were almost locked but I got them going again. Near the top, some forty feet from the ground, a bolt was loose in its bed and the pipe started pulling away. The creeper's nightmare. Flinging up a long arm I grabbed the guttering without putting too much strain on it and carefully pulled myself up, distributing leverage where I could. The bag flapping between my legs didn't help but I managed to reach and pull myself on to the roof.

I was on the inner angle with a view of other roofs at varying heights shining like gunmetal under a too-bright moon. Chimney stacks stuck up from the irregular mass like periscopes. This time, as I wanted to cover a fair distance silently but with speed, I sat on the sloping roof with my knees up so that I could use both feet and hands to suction on to the tiles as I worked my way along. The knack is to keep the back straight and not look down. The only quicker way is to straddle the angle of the rooftop, which meant putting myself on view against the skyline.

It was three o'clock in the morning and London was a black box with yellow pinholes. By keeping my legs together as I moved I was able to cradle the bag to stop it banging. The varying roof heights caused problems and I climbed up and down narrow stacks, using fire escapes where I could, rejoicing over the few flat tops that I could walk straight across. When I reached Reisen's I knew. The evil feel of it came right up through the tiles, trying alternately to hurl me off or draw me in.

Locating the down hole in the gutters, I performed a couple of tortuous movements that brought me on to the stack, then took stock of the nearest window. There was no tributary pipe here so I put an ankle lock on the pipe while I used my pencil torch. It was a risk I couldn't avoid.

Disgusted with my own lack of preparation, I flashed the light around the frame without finding obvious alarms. Had there been I'm not sure what I'd have done for I couldn't have removed the frame from my very precarious position with the tools I had. There could be a vibrator alarm, of course, reacting when a pane was broken. There was only one way to find out. By reaching across, holding the pipe with feet and one hand, I used my glass cutter along the window base and then semi-circled above it. A sharp tap and the piece of glass fell through. I now had somewhere to grab if I slipped.

Climbing up a notch or two I made another cut on the upper pane and after pushing it through jabbed with the cutter to remove any jagged pieces. Grabbing the woodwork in the gap I swung over, pulling myself up on one arm and getting fingertip purchase on the top of the frame with my free hand, then rammed a foot in the lower pane aperture. I was standing upright on the window, which was an old-fashioned sash type with a catch holding the two frames.

Opening the catch with my penknife was no problem and pulling the upper frame down was easy. I then climbed into the room, pushed the top frame back up and raised the lower frame so that I could dive for the pipe if I had to. It was all much too easy and if I hadn't realized it before I was thinking now that it was all a waste of time. Either Reisen kept nothing here and so didn't give a damn who climbed in or he was expecting me.

I didn't rate my chances but had to go through the motions. The room was a small office with two desks and a typewriter. A quick look in the desk drawers convinced me that this was Penny's office. When I tried one of the two doors it was locked and I had to fiddle a bit before I could open it. It led into the reception room. The door from the reception room which led into Reisen's office was also locked; a double mortice which took a little time. Eventually the door swung back. A patch of grey light showed up the window at the far end of the room.

Closing the door behind me. I stepped across the thick pile and unlocked the intercommunicating door leading back to Penny's office; otherwise my opened window would be useless to me. As Reisen's window faced the street I dared not open it as the fuzz might see it.

I then faced the expanse of Reisen's gaudy, vulgar office. Where should I start? A little speculation might save me a lot of work so I sat down in Reisen's chair and was immediately aware of his presence. Maybe sitting in his seat would help me think his way. I put the bag on the desk and tried to work it out.

The office stretched ahead of me, dark hunks of furniture standing out against the lighter shadows of walls and carpet. It was crazy to come here. I gazed round at walls, floor and ceiling, wondering where I would hide stuff that must stay hidden from any form of search.

The carpet could hide a lot but a full-scale police search would have it up so I ruled that out. Walls would be searched and tapped. Desk minutely examined for secret drawers. Chairs examined for possible cavities. Every inch would be searched. So what am I doing here? Well, I'm a creeper not a cop; I'd been faced with hiding things myself.

I went over to the window where he kept his war photographs and medal and had a feeling of being warm. Examining the photos left me no wiser, yet, inexplicably, I felt they played a part. Tapping the wall beneath and below the window achieved nothing but sore knuckles. A panelled radiator beneath the window-ledge was cold. For a while I played around with the radiator control thinking it might operate a panel, but nothing happened. Carefully peering outside the window I noticed a broad stone sill with a long window-box hooked to it. The nape of my neck prickled and I wondered if I dare raise the window.

I didn't dare use my torch around the frame, so my sensitive fingertips searched for any form of alarm. I found two. All I now had to do was to find the switch and the most likely place was somewhere around the desk or the main door. Suddenly I was optimistic, the scent strong in my nostrils.

My torch flashed its string beam round the desk and I located the switch under the kneehole, a plastic flex, desk colour, running down to disappear through the carpet. It had to be the right switch with the way things were beginning to run for me. On hands and knees I craned to read the markings. *On* in red, *Off* in black. Common enough. But if the markings meant anything the alarm was already switched off. I steadied like a pointer. My own alarms began to ring. Switched off?

I backed out from the kneehole and half-rose as the room filled with shadows. Two smudges of grey light showed open doors and I turned like a terrier to dive for the window, already knowing that it was useless. The torch was still on, the beam flicking across the room as I sped forward. They brought me down and my outstretched hands knocked the photos from the window ledge. As I crashed I twisted my body so that I landed on the back of my shoulders. The torchlight flashed madly across the ceiling, lighting the chandeliers into crazy prisms which danced off the droppers and on to walls and ceiling; a brief impression embedded into my mind at the most crucial moment.

Every trick I had ever learned, including some I had vowed never to use, flowed from my feet, knees, elbows, hands, teeth and head. I put up the fight of my life and the room was filled with sickening sounds and foul language. But how can you beat half a dozen men who have the drop on you? They beat me to slow unconsciousness. I don't think I was out for long; they wanted me awake.

My face felt a mess as my eyes flickered open. There was no point in pretence so I pulled round as soon as a throbbing head would let me. There was blood in my mouth and I could feel its slow trickle from my nose. The lights were on, the heavy drapes drawn as I slowly took stock. I'd over-estimated myself; there were five of them, not including Rexy, who wouldn't have bruised his hands on me. In spite of their leers I could see that I'd done damage. I hadn't done so badly but not nearly good enough.

Knocker Roberts was the only one without a smile. There wasn't a mark on his face that hadn't been there before. Spitting blood over the plush carpet I said good evening to one and all and gave a hopeful tug at the rope that fixed me to the chair.

Reisen was sitting on the edge of his desk, arms folded, for once without a cigar, and with a fixed grin on his thin face. I had made his day. The mean-looking character I had seen with Knocker the last time here had a half-closed eye and a jagged scar down his cheek where one of my nails must have carved him. I could see he didn't like me even before he drew the razor from his pocket. He advanced on me with hate and an open blade.

'Lay off,' said Knocker.

Mean-Face scowled. 'Rex said it was all right to carve him before dropping him in the bucket so why should you worry?'

'Cut it out,' said Knocker again. He said it wearily but there was a peculiar power that made Reisen look over to him, then eye Mean-Face who was torn between the two. Reisen came down on Knocker's side because he needed him more than the other bloke. 'OK. Leave him.' The razor disappeared.

'Thanks, Knock,' I mumbled, not wanting to embarrass him.

Knocker gazed bleakly at me, the shutters up. 'That's all I can do, whack. You're for the drop.'

'How did you know I was coming?' I asked Reisen reasonably.

He looked around at the others, grinning, showing how clever he was.

'Because I know every bloody thing, don't I? That's why I'm here.' He laughed. 'It was all that was left for you to do, wasn't it? I knew you wouldn't leave your home patch. So I made it easy for you, Spider. You're a good creeper, though, mate. I'll give you that. I'll be sorry to see you go but you know how it is? Grassers must all go the same way and you cost me a packet. Take him down.'

About to yell out I was sapped from behind and adhesive tape was stuck over my mouth. I gave them dead weight all the way down the stairs to the ground floor. Someone checked that the street was clear, then four of them carried me to a car while I tried to struggle but with little strength. All four got in the car and off we went.

We drove to a street somewhere south of the Thames. One side was a factory wall and on the other early Victorian terraced houses in a state of rapid decay. It was utterly silent except for a lapping of the river somewhere near. They dragged me down the basement steps of a derelict house and into a cellar, which, as Tilley lamps were lit, was obviously used as a torture chamber.

I was strapped into something like an electric chair. Reisen had now arrived with Knocker and the door was locked and bolted. The window had been blacked-out with baffleboard.

Reisen was still grinning, highly satisfied with his perception and its effect on his subordinates. Knocker was grim-faced but I knew there'd be no further help from him. Reisen pulled viciously at the tape over my mouth and as it came away it ripped some skin. But that was the least of my worries. Spitting more blood I noticed that the concrete floor was already bloodstained from some other poor wretch.

'You can shout as much as you like here, Spider,' said Reisen affably. 'The walls and ceiling have been insulated and the house is empty. So give it a go, mate, relieve yourself if it helps.'

The only thing I had left was self-respect and God knows why I clung on to it. I just wouldn't let someone like Reisen see how desperately scared I was.

'Aren't you going to explain why you involved me in all this? Let's face it, I can't tell anyone now, can I?'

'That's right, Spider, you can't. Not even old Davey Jones.' He continued grinning but I had the feeling that it was all an act for the boys. 'I'm just not a talker,' Reisen continued. 'If you haven't worked it out for yourself there's no point in telling you at this stage. Ignorance is bliss, ain't it?'

A shallow metal tray with collapsible sides was shoved under my feet, then the sides were raised and locked. I got the message and the sweat flowed. In spite of myself I struggled in terror but the clamps on my arms and legs were so tight and firm that I could barely move my fingers and toes.

'Take it easy, whack. It won't do no good.' Knocker offered compassion. Had it been anyone else he would have enjoyed himself but he was probably remembering how I had helped him in nick. The concrete had already been mixed and they started spreading it around my feet up to ankle level.

I kept wriggling my feet in the vain hope of creating a cavity through which I could slip them, but the concrete came creeping back each time and my ankles began to tire. In any event I could not have pulled my feet out once the concrete had set. Yet I kept it up to the point of exhaustion because it was all that was left for me to do.

When the tray was full Reisen said, 'It's quick setting. We must drop before dawn. I won't be seeing you again, Spider, so while you're all alone remember that two million quid went down the pan. What you're getting is too good, boy.'

He turned away, and about to call him a murderous bastard I had a desperate idea and bit back the words in time.

'Get Penny down here,' I bawled. 'I was with her and couldn't have followed Knocker.'

Reisen half-turned his back towards me. 'She'd have told me before. It's no go, Spider.'

'She's afraid of you, for Christ's sake. It's my bloody life you're playing with. Get her here. *Get her.*'

Reisen hesitated and Knocker said, 'I'll get her. Half an hour at the most.' He didn't wait for Reisen's permission and I reflected that Knocker had come up better than I could expect. Reisen walked across the cellar and sat on a plank on trestles. The others fell back as he had. He refrained from smoking, he didn't want to drop identifying ash. He seemed to lose interest in me.

If Knocker's Aston Martin was around on the empty streets he'd be back on time but it was my last fling. It was a long half-hour and I reckon I lost weight during it. Nobody spoke at all while Knocker was absent and the silence was like a graveyard. And I supposed that I was as good as in one.

When Knocker returned he was pulling a dishevelled Penny clad in a diaphanous short nightie and negligée. She was white and afraid and I could guess that Knocker had stood no nonsense when she had almost certainly refused to come. She looked at everyone bar me as if I was a blind spot in her vision. Even without make-up she gave the boys a treat and they all focused on her with varying degrees of interest.

Reisen spoke quietly. 'Spider here says he was with you at the time Knocker reckons he was being tailed by him. Just tell the truth, love.'

I had to admit that Reisen kept threat from his tone but it all depended on her knowledge of him and the depth of her fear. She stood there staring wide-eyed at Reisen, so I yelled :

'What's the matter with you? Can't you face me? Can't you look at what you've done? Tell the truth for God's sake.'

She turned so slowly that I thought she would never make it. There were fatigue smudges under her eyes as they furtively met mine. Seeing me like this must surely stir her. But she stared with half-vacant eyes that barely recognized me. She was in fear for herself.

'Tell them,' I coaxed with quiet desperation. 'Tell them we were together.'

He gaze dropped to the concrete pad and something moved in her. Perhaps she saw herself in my place and her fear deepened to terror. 'He wasn't with me,' she jerked out and walked slowly towards the door. For once in her life she had told the truth and pulled the trigger.

'OK. Put the lamps out.' Reisen rose abruptly and it was all over.

I wanted to yell at her again, plead for compassion, but had seized up. When I tried to shout my larynx contracted and I almost choked myself. Before I could moisten my mouth to try again Mean-Face taped my lips for no other reason than it gave him pleasure. The Tilley lamps were doused. I heard the retreating footsteps, the opening and closing of the door and finally the key turning in the lock.

The only sound left was my own frantic heartbeat. A gurgle crept through my lips as I tried to move the tape.

Desperately I worked my feet again but it was already more difficult and I knew that there was no escape. This was it. The terrifying moment of facing a particularly nasty death and all I could do was to dwell on it in the darkest room I had known. This was the worst part, the torture, the pounding blackness that robbed my senses and disorientated me except for the gradual hardening of the concrete over my feet. It was all intended as part of the punishment and now they weren't here I thought to hell with self-respect.

And despair gushed out in several forms but there was no one to see, no one to pity or help me. I wanted to cry but fear had dehydrated me and I could feel the dampness of my clothes. The pain from the roughing-up in Reisen's office was nothing to the empty darkness. The deep silence rolled through my mind, which was on the verge of abject panic.

Oh, Maggie, Maggie, I thought. Just to see your sweet face once more. Just once. But it was too late to think of Maggie. It was better that she didn't know how I had let her down. And it was much too late to regret meeting Penny. Maybe it would have made no difference; Reisen would have found another way. I would just have liked to have seen Maggie from a distance, without her knowing, to say I was sorry without her hearing. Instead I said it almost inaudibly to the bare, dark walls. Maggie always came to mind when I hit trouble, like a prayer being answered. I thanked God she would be spared the agony of knowing how it ended for me.

Then I began to face it slowly. Then to accept it. I stopped the futile wriggling of my feet which by this time was largely imaginary anyway. It didn't make me feel better, but it calmed me. Finally, all I wanted was a little light to disperse the shadows. By the time the execution party returned I was a limp zombie, completely reconciled to what they were going to do. When Knocker lit a Tilley lamp and peered at me, he obviously thought my mind had gone. In a way it had.

'Don't worry, whack. We'll be as quick as we can.' A touch of sentimentality from Knocker. A promise to kill speedily.

In a light-headed moment I wanted to laugh but all I could do was blink blindly at the light.

They were careful when they unstrapped my arms but I'd lost most of my circulation and there was little I could do. The struggle I attempted was pathetic so my hands were tied behind my back just in case I made a last-minute effort. The sides of the container were released by practical fingers. The concrete block was not large but heavy enough to take me all the way to the bottom unhindered by any action I might make with my arms. The final indignity was when I was lifted on to a trolley like a sack of coal and wheeled over to the door. After due precaution they carried me up to the street. There were now only four of them and I noted that my old friend the grey van had been brought back into action.

They dumped me in an awkward and painful position. What was a little more pain? I rolled about as the van got under way and a couple of the boys started to jibe at me until Knocker stopped them.

We didn't go far. When we stopped they waited a while to be certain that the area was deserted. It was now about five in the morning and chilly. They lugged me on to the pavement and I recognized Waterloo Bridge, empty and unfriendly at this hour. They wanted to finish the job quickly before the fuzz came round on patrol. Hoisting me on to the balustrade was quite a job. All I could do was to wriggle and retard them but they finally got me up with my feet overhanging the river, the weight of the concrete almost pulling me down of its own accord. I pushed back with all my strength against arms preparing to throw me as I saw the rising water, black and oily below me and I struggled like a maniac against their pressure. It was a long drop down. The rope was cut from my wrists but they were holding me fast, prepared for a struggle.

I started to slide as someone yelled, 'There's a car,' and grabbed me.

'Get rid of him quick for Christ's sake.' It was Mean-Face panicking.

Then Knocker snarled, 'Hold him. It's Rex's car.' And somehow they drew me back. Turning my head to avoid the frightening effect of looking down I saw the car racing up the bridge, its headlamps flashing signals I did not understand, but it stopped the others from pushing me over.

The car skidded to a halt just behind the van and Reisen flew out yelling, 'Get him back in the van. Move, blast you.'

I almost vomited in relief. They pulled me back until I was standing on the pavement like a toy soldier with a lead base. Reisen himself tore open the van doors and I was carried in and laid flat.

Reisen bent over me and grasped my right hand between both of his. I thought I'd gone round the bend because he kept pumping my hand and I swear that there were tears in his eyes. 'Forgive me, Spider. Forgive me, boy.' There was a catch in his voice. The others stood around the van and he turned and snarled at them like an aimal. 'Get out while I'm talking to my mate. We nearly made a terrible mistake.'

When they had gone he patted my face like an old friend. 'We'll soon have that stuff off your feet. Then a bath up at my place, eh? Breakfast. Eggs and bacon and hot coffee, eh? Just the job. We've got to stick together, you and me, eh? Difficult jobs ours. People don't understand. I'll have you right, Spider old friend. Don't you worry about a thing.'

I could only stare in wonderment. Maybe I *had* drowned and this was an after-life.

When I opened the door to my pad I was only half-surprised to see the bowler hat and umbrella on the bed. Fairfax was sitting in my favourite chair smoking a cigar, a good deal of ash already in the airline giveaway ashtray he had raked out. He held the cigar very differently from Reisen; he was born with one in his mouth. I felt a queer mixture of pleasure and annoyance at seeing his straight back and immaculate figure so out of place in this room.

'You've nicked my chair,' I protested as I closed the door behind me.

'Only because I knew that you would have offered it to me had you been here. You've been a hell of a time.'

We were back to normal – our love-hate relationship as if we met daily. Ours was the most unlikely association imaginable. We sprang from opposite ends of the social scale. His position was such that at this stage there need be no personal contact. Yet there were moments of affinity between us that were puzzling to both. And there were still debts to be settled, points of honour important to us both.

'I was out for a swim,' I flung at him casually, sitting in the only chair left. He was as I remembered, lean-faced and impassive, grey hair well-brushed, eyebrows giving rein to his only facial expression.

'I know,' he said drily. 'It was I who threw the lifebelt.'

I stared at him long and angrily. 'You knew that Reisen was topping me?'

'How else could I have dissuaded him?'

I sprang to my feet and shouted in pure anger. 'Well, you left it bloody late then, didn't you? Christ, I was nearly in the bloody drink.'

'Calm down, Spider. For God's sake sit down. Why must you always explode?'

I was just about to tell him through a constricted throat and mounting blood pressure when he waved a restraining hand.

'You went off at a tangent. We had difficulty tracing you. In fact we didn't find you. However, at that stage it was obvious what was happening to you. I had to make direct contact with Reisen, and that took time because he too had temporarily disappeared. But here you are, fit and well and smelling like a desert brothel.'

I began to relax. 'Reisen insisted that I used his aftershave. Well, what have you been up to, you crafty old bugger?'

'I really don't know why I bother with you, Spider. I should have thought it obvious why Reisen used you.'

'I have some ideas. What are yours?'

He looked carefully at me, giving nothing away by expression and establishing the difference between us. 'We knew from the outset that Reisen had been paid highly to spring Alan Bruce Chapman. He did it well, but his character would not permit Chapman's ultimate removal to Moscow. So he had to dream up a scheme that would satisfy the Russians. A scapegoat was desirable. None came better than in the form of Willie "Spider" Scott.' He smiled bleakly. 'After all, wasn't Reisen convinced that you had friends in high places?

'So he involved you in Chapman's escape in such a way that you were bound, eventually, to report Chapman's whereabouts. He knew that you could not tolerate a traitor, even as he, in his twisted way, could not. Then when Chapman was recaptured any investigation would lead back to you. All the arrows pointed your way, all those towards Reisen having been carefully obliterated. Your agency even arranged the air passage. He relied on your influence in high places to deal with the situation.'

'I had reckoned that much,' I said. 'So what went wrong?'

Fairfax answered carefully and I wasn't sure that I was getting the whole truth. 'There were areas of government authority who did not want Chapman recaptured. Prison was too accessible to a determined operator who, over the course of time, could extract a good deal from him. So knowing that your misguided loyalties would keep you from telling the police, I removed all other methods of communication from your reach. I could not be contacted.'

'Thanks very much. Bloody typical. I had ulcers trying to trace you and do the right thing.'

'I applaud your zeal but it had to be that way. Reisen had to go through with the escape plans. He cleverly used them as a distraction for a drug robbery. But he had banked on your having informed authority and that Chapman would be arrested. If he was not, then Reisen had at least tried and his peculiar conscience would have been partially appeased. He had manoeuvred you to the airport at the time of Chapman's flight as another little enmeshing trick should it be needed. I gather that you drove the getaway van.'

'You gather what you like. Who shot Chapman?'

'I'll come to that. Reisen had intended you to inform on Chapman but grassing on a good deal of stolen opium was another matter. *That* was not on the agenda. As I had withdrawn my advice when you tried so hard to contact me I felt a certain responsibility towards you.'

'So you told Rexy boy to lay off and he did. Cried over me like a brother.'

'In a sense he thinks he is. I merely told him, Spider, that I do not have to act within the law. That if I wanted to do him damage I do not require judge and jury. I assured him that you did not inform but that I knew who did. I informed him that you were in a very special position involving national interest and that there was a part to play for him.'

'You what?' I yelled, disbelieving it.

Fairfax rolled off cigar ash with a fastidious movement of his fingers. He was quite serious when he met my gaze. 'As I understand it,' he continued, 'Reisen's big frustration in life is lack of real and recognized heroism; a man who many times dreams of winning the Victoria Cross, thus winning public acclaim. I merely appealed to this secret ambition. To save you, my dear fellow, I've convinced him that he's on the strength, a government agent. Unpaid, of course; he does not need the money.'

Fairfax paused and the corners of his mouth twitched. Was it the beginning of a smile that old Straight-Back was showing? 'I congratulated him on removing Chapman from the scene,' he added.

I was beginning to see the funny side of this. 'He didn't knock off Chapman and you know it.'

'Of course. He was on the point of denying it but as there were only the two of us with no witnesses he suddenly saw the stupendous glory of admitting it. Reisen had arrived at last. He couldn't talk about his secret, but *he knew*, don't you see, that he had saved this old country by assassinating a traitor and that I believed it and to him this was tremendously important. What an incredibly complex character!'

I laughed and it did me good but Fairfax controlled himself beautifully, for ever the straight man.

'I really must find a special medal for him. I must look in my diddy-box.'

Fairfax rose and retrieved his umbrella and hat. I believe I detected a spark behind the ice of his eyes. 'I think that squares us beautifully, Spider. Knock for knock.' He was alluding to the Chinese affair. 'You ought to get a better room than this. You can surely afford it?'

'Who knocked off Chapman?' I insisted.

'Haven't I just told you?'

'Nuts.'

'The Russians then?'

'Nuts to that too.'

'Then I've no idea.' He walked to the door.

'One reason you didn't answer my calls was that you wanted no possible evidence of anyone having informed you of Chapman's whereabouts. Officially you didn't want to know where he was. You sent the Special Branch so that you could prove, if necessary, that you had tried to make contact with me. But you knew that I wouldn't speak to coppers. *You* had him knocked off.'

He turned to face me but I had not expected a reaction.

'Maggie's back soon, isn't she?' he asked politely.

I nodded.

'Good. She'll keep you out of mischief. You shouldn't really have turned down the offer I made to you before. Oh, and the champagne is on you this time. Vintage, of course. Good day to you.'

The smooth old bastard raised his hat and was gone. Maybe Chapman was better off where he was. I know I am.